The I

The Lake

Living A Meaningful Life

by
Brian Hunter

Published by
Wizard Way
Rainbow Wisdom
Ireland

Copyright © 2022 Brian Hunter

All rights reserved.
No part of this publication may be reproduced, stored in a retrieval system, or transmitted, in any form or by any means, electronic, mechanical, photocopying, recording or otherwise without the prior permission of *Rainbow Wisdom*

This book is sold subject to the condition that it shall not, by way of trade or otherwise, be lent, re-sold, hired out, or otherwise circulated without the publisher's prior consent in any form of binding or cover other than that in which it is published and without a similar condition including this condition being imposed on the subsequent purchaser.

Names have been modified in the book to protect the identities of certain individuals. Others are included with full permission. While others are too strongly recognized by universal consciousness to be concealed.

ISBN: 9798794368796

DEDICATION

This book is dedicated to all of those who have failed at something but didn't give up. Also dedicated to those who have provided help and inspiration to others in urging them not to give up.

CONTENTS

	PREFACE ……………………………….	8
1	The Storm …………………………….	9
2	The Mistake. …………..............……………….	53
3	The Visitations ……………………………............	75
4	The Redemption ……….…………….............	105
	Acknowledgments…………………..............…	134
	About The Author………………………..........	135
	Also, by Brian Hunter ……………...............…	136
	Living A Meaningful Life: Series Synopsis....	141

PREFACE

The Lake is Book #3 in the series, "Living A Meaningful Life," by Brian Hunter. *The Lake* is a highly meaningful and entertaining book in its' own right. But to better understand some of the storylines, back-stories, and context, it is highly recommended that you first read Books #1 & #2:

      Book #1: ***The Bench: Living A Meaningful Life***
      Book #2: ***The Farm: Living A Meaningful Life***

CHAPTER ONE

The Storm

By some miracle, I had endured and survived another year of school, and at the notoriously brutal Carlisle High School, no less. I was looking forward to a quiet summer spent at home and at the park with friends, or perhaps just sitting alone on the bench, contemplating my increasingly complicated 'non-life,' as I had begun to call it.

The incredible experience I had enjoyed at Frank's farm during a previous summer had faded from my mind a bit. Yes, I still retained all of those memories, skills, and lessons I took from my amazing time there, but a year of school has a way of stripping away any and all humanity within a person. I had grown cynical of people, teenagers especially, and had once again tried to become more invisible, rather than taking a more leadership role in life, such as I did at the farm.

I guess you could say that school was not good for me. My time at the farm, for example, allowed me to make great strides toward becoming an actual decent person (maybe?); but then after a couple months of school, my soul would turn black and stone-like from all of the toxicity, while the "system" of condescending robot-like treatment of students would turn me back into a "child," that was to only remain silent and do what he was told.

However, even as I describe school as being the third level of Hell, I also liked school at the same time. I was a good student, and I liked being good at *something*. I was terrible at sports, I was not very popular with the girls, and I was not very popular at all, in general.

We will define "popular" as having others look upon you in a very positive, likeable, and fun way. I was a bit "popular," but not in *that* way. My version of "popular" was that people liked to listen to rumors about me, make up rumors about me, and spread rumors about me. Mostly, there were rumors about my connections to the "adult world." There were whispers about how weird I had been in spending so much time with the "mysterious grumpy old man," who was actually the nicest old man I had ever known, Mr. Wilkens. Additionally, there were rumors about my strong relationship with Frank at the farm, and how I had been a leader of sorts while there. A person might ask how any of this is bad. The answer is simple. I was being labeled a "child-adult."

What I mean by "child-adult" is that I did not have the respect of an adult because I wasn't an adult. But then it was also not looked upon positively by some that I was acting, or being, an adult to a large degree. In other words, I had slipped between the cracks into nowhere land, where I was not an adult, but I was also not like all the other kids. This made me feel lonely. But at the same time, I also felt special in some way.

It is difficult when you start to become an older teenager in high school, and you are wanting to fit into a group of your peers, and be accepted. I was gradually seeing that I would never fit into a normal group of my peers. I was always going to be in a 'group' consisting of only myself. This created conflict within me though, between accepting and embracing this fate, or fighting against it, and trying stuff myself down onto a level where I could be a normal kid, with normal friends, doing normal things for kids my age.

Deep down inside, I had a feeling I could not explain, which was that I had an important destiny to fulfill. However, I also felt a rebellious pull to turn my back on it, and enjoy the carefree recklessness that kids my age normally enjoyed. The funny thing about destiny and fate though, is that once it grabs you, it often never lets go. I was not going to escape my destiny, and this was going to be the summer that showed me this.

It all started when my mom came up to my room to talk with me. My mom informed me that she had heard from Frank at the farm. Frank was "suggesting," and "offering," that I attend the special camp at "The Lake." I was a bit surprised by this offer. I had kind of expected Frank to try and get me to go back to the farm. I knew Frank liked me, and my time there had been very successful and meaningful. I naturally assumed he would want me to come back. However, as usual, it was a mistake to ASSUME anything with Frank.

Frank told my mother he felt it would be very beneficial for me to "experience," or "enjoy," some time at The Lake. In "Frank language," this meant that Frank felt there were things I had to learn, and I would learn them at The Lake. My mother saw it differently. My mother saw it as an excuse to get me out of the house for a period of time. Knowing my mother would think this way, Frank also sweetened the deal by telling my mother that my time at The Lake would be free of charge.

At the time, I was not sure how Frank could have arranged for this. I thought Frank was just involved with the farm. I didn't think he had anything to do with The Lake. Frank actually owned the farm himself. However, The Lake was owned and operated by The Carlisle Trust.

The Carlisle Trust was a very huge and wealthy non-profit organization set up by the Carlisles many years ago, for the benefit of our community, and especially all of the kids in the area. The Carlisle Trust, or "The Trust" as some people called it, owned many properties all over the area. One of them was this very large and sprawling lake camp/beach/resort type thing that was located outside of town on the largest lake in our tri-state area.

The Lake was open during the summer only. It had lodges that people could rent, a few restaurants and shops, lots of concession stands, and a huge beach that stretched quite a long distance, and was adjacent to undeveloped wilderness. This allowed for a section to be used as a public beach, but there were also areas for a couple different youth summer camps. There was a camp for young kids, and another for teens.

The camps, and everything else at The Lake, were really nice. The Trust maintained everything in great condition, and had invested in sailboats and other fun things that could be rented by the public, or used by the campers. Although The Carlisle Trust, who owned all of this, was a non-profit, they obviously had to charge for the use of everything as a way of paying the huge expenses associated with such an operation. Thus, camps at The Lake were very expensive. Most of the time, kids who went there came from well-off families, although The Trust did offer some scholarships to allow more equal access.

SO, my mother was THRILLED by the offer of me attending The Lake at no cost to her. This was seen as a big win by her, and indeed it was. It was a winning opportunity, and it was very generous of Frank to somehow arrange this. Don't get me wrong, I didn't want to seem ungrateful. It's just that I wanted to stay home and relax. Or in other words, I wanted to remain inside my bedroom, in denial of my reality. That reality being the need for me to further develop and grow to be ready for what life was going to be throwing at me.

Anyway, my mother, very excited, finished her presentation on what a wonderful opportunity this was. I had remained silent. I'm guessing she could tell by my underwhelming reaction that I was not as excited as her. My mother told me to just think about it, and we would discuss it again later.

I did think about it. At first, I was leaning toward "no," but then I thought more about it. To be honest, there were only two factors that changed my mind toward attending. Firstly, the fact that the "offer," translated as "request," for me to attend, came from Frank, weighed heavily upon me. I respected Frank more than my parents. One thing my mother never realized was that although I did not always do what SHE requested, I most certainly did everything Frank requested. Frank was my mentor. In fact, since my time at the farm with him, I had gone back at various times just to sit and milk cows with him so that we could chat. I trusted him, and I also wanted him to respect me, and be approving of my life choices. I knew if Frank wanted me to go, this meant I would have to go. But my mother did not have to know this, and I would still negotiate my best deal for going.

The second factor that convinced me to consider going, was a "condition," translated as "demand," that would have to be met in order for me to agree to attend. I went downstairs to speak with my mother about my thoughts and my condition for attending.

I told my mom that if Frank wanted me to go to The Lake, that I would go. However, I would only go under one condition. My mom anxiously asked me what it was. I said to her, "I want Eric to go with me."

I had met Eric at the farm, and we became best friends. Eric lived in a different area, and he didn't go to my school, but we were still able to maintain our friendship. Perhaps this lake thing was going to be a way of hanging out with Eric again. That was very appealing to me.

However, my "condition" was met with a very stern look from my mother. She said, "Oh come on! You know Eric's mom can't afford to send him to The Lake." She added, "Frank's offer was for you only. It was not for anyone else."

I replied to her, "Well, can't you just ask Frank if Eric can receive the offer also?"

My mom huffed like I had just insulted her. She said, "THAT WOULD BE RUDE! When someone offers you something very generous, you can't then ask if you can have another, or more, or for your friends also. WHAT IS WRONG WITH YOU?"

I knew what she was getting at. Under normal circumstances my mom was right. I was not a total idiot or social misfit. However, I felt I could make this happen. I just had this feeling that this was totally doable.

I said to my mom, "Can you just mention to Frank that I feel it is important that Eric receive this opportunity also?"

I added, "This way, it is not YOU being rude. It's coming from me."

My mom looked very agitated and said, "Well I think you are out of line asking Frank for this, but I will tell him what you just said."

I replied, "That's all I ask."

I know my mom left our conversation being absolutely certain that my request was ridiculous, and would be denied by Frank. I left the conversation knowing that Eric would be coming with me to The Lake.

The next day, my mom came into my room and said, "I spoke to Frank."

I replied, "Yeah, what did he say?"

She said, "He said that if you felt strongly about Eric going, that is good enough for him, and that he will speak with Eric's mom and make it happen."

My mom had this cross and irritated look on her face, because she always hated being wrong, and she hated even more when I was right. I only replied to her, "Yep, good."

My mom stared at me for a moment and said, "I have no idea how you are able to get all of these adults running around in circles for you."

I simply replied, "Because they know I am willing to run around in circles for them."

My mom shook her head in irritated disbelief and walked out of my room.

It was on! I was going to The Lake! And I was going with my best friend Eric!

On a beautiful sunny Saturday morning, my mom dropped me off at The Lake. There were no protests from me this time, and there were no tears of sadness from me this time. I was excited! Mostly, I was excited to see Eric. I knew I would do some fun stuff at the lake camp, but really, I just wanted to hang out with my best friend, and perhaps fully enjoy the summer after all.

I said goodbye to my mom, and she drove off. I went directly to the camp office with my suitcase. I knew the man in charge, and he knew me. He was an older man named Benny. I knew Benny from school. While Benny ran all of the operations at The Lake during the summer, he was also part of the coaching staff within the Athletics Department at Carlisle High School during the school year. The school moved him around a lot depending on the need, but he was mostly known as a swim coach and one of the track coaches.

Benny was known as a tough man, but a good man. Anyone who has ever been in very competitive high school sports, knows that this is the perfect type of coach. They MUST be very tough and cut nobody any breaks, BUT they must also possess this sense of goodness, which is what makes all the athletes love their coach, even if the coach is brutal with them. It's an interesting combination, and a difficult balance, but Benny did this very well, and he was much respected by the kids and the community.

Specifically, the fact he was the Director of Operations at The Lake, showed he had the total confidence of The Carlisle Trust, and this was not easy to earn. Most everyone who had important positions within The Trust, usually had a prior relationship with the Carlisles in some way, or were close to someone who did. Like Frank, Benny had a personal tie with the Carlisles that went way back. All I know for sure is that Mrs. Carlisle herself, had relied upon Benny for various responsibilities after George Carlisle had passed away many years ago.

Benny saw me walking into the office, and he came to greet me. His first words to me were, "You must be pretty important for everyone above me to want you here." But then he added, "However, now that you are here, you're mine, and you shouldn't expect this to be all easy-street young man."

That was a little more harsh than I expected, and I replied, "Yes, Sir, but I am looking forward to enjoying myself at camp here."

Benny just laughed. (Ominous?)

Then he said, "Okay Sport, let me show you to your accommodations." He went on to say, "I am only sticking you in with one other camper, and I think you know him."

I replied, "Yes, Sir. Excellent!"

I followed him out of the office and down a walkway to where most of the camp-lodging was. We went into a lodge that was right up front, facing the lake. He took me down the hallway to the end, and opened the door to where I would be staying. As he did so, he quipped, "Here is your premium VIP room, Sir," and he laughed.

His remark was both sarcastic and true at the same time. While it was a very small, bland, dormitory style room with nothing more than two uncomfortable looking bunks, a table, and a tiny bathroom, it was truly one of the "premium" rooms, because it was a double room with its own bathroom, AND a VIEW of the lake. Most of the rooms for campers were stuffed with four kids, did not have their own bathroom (they had to use the ones in the hallways), and there was no view. So even though Benny was able to turn it into sarcasm, it was clear that someone had indeed instructed him to give us one of the best rooms.

Did I say "US?" YES I DID! More importantly than the details of the accommodations, was the fact that Eric was already in the room getting settled into his bunk. We both smiled at each other and hugged. Benny said, "Well isn't this cute and sweet," in his tough-guy sarcastic tone, even though he probably did think it was cute and sweet. He added, "When you boys are ready, come over to the office, and I will fill you in on all the details of everything we have to offer here, including food, as I'm sure you are hungry."

Eric and I thanked him, and he left. Eric and I made some small-talk to get reacquainted. Eric had already claimed the top bunk, but only because he knew I would prefer the bottom one. Eric was so predictably nice and easy to get along with. However, unlike at the farm, I would be treating Eric as an equal this time, and I would be trying to make sure his preferences were respected as much as mine, if not more so.

Eric and I were wanting to talk and get caught up with life, but we could see through our window how nice and sunny it was outside. Plus, the lake looked incredibly inviting with the sun glistening on the slight ripples. Thus, we decided to take our conversation outside.

We left the lodge (I should just call it a dormitory, but we'll keep with "lodge"). We both were taking a long look around us. All we could see was a sand beach that stretched beyond our sight, lots of kids playing, lots of adults relaxing, lots of staff scurrying around, a very nice collection of sailboats that The Lake had available for rent or use by campers, and most dramatic of all, the lake. The lake was HUGE. It was so vast, you could not see the other side. Between the lake being so enormous, and the beach stretching for such a long distance, it gave one the feeling of being at the ocean. But nope, it was the largest freshwater lake in the area, and it was by far the largest beach in the area. It was an incredible piece of property.

The story behind it, was that George Carlisle had purchased it shortly before his retirement. He originally planned on dividing it up into lake-front house lots. However, as his ambition started to wane before retirement, he started looking at things differently. The story goes, that Mr. Carlisle decided that instead of having only a handful of elite people enjoying the property, instead he would turn it into a public establishment so that EVERYONE from near and far could come and enjoy the property. Thus, instead of selling it all off in pieces, he decided to transfer it to The Carlisle Trust.

His vision of everyone from near and far enjoying it turned out to be accurate. The Lake had always been viewed as the most epic summer spot in the state, and including the adjacent states as well. I would say that besides the high school, which George Carlisle built, The Lake is probably one of his largest and most well-known legacies. This is why Benny being put in charge of the whole thing was as much of an honor as it was a job for him. The Lake was definitely the "flagship" of The Carlisle Trust holdings.

As I was looking around and taking everything in, I was wondering why in the world Frank thought it was so important for me to spend time here. Don't get me wrong, I was grateful, and this was starting to look like some kind of reward, or nice gesture for me to enjoy. BUT, Frank was usually not one to hand out "rewards." Frank was the type of person to offer an opportunity to EARN a reward. Thus, I remained puzzled as to why I was really here.

Regardless of that, I was going to simply enjoy myself. I was also questioning how incredibly stupid I was for even considering not coming here. *WHAT WAS I THINKING?* Did I really think playing dead in my bedroom all summer was a better choice than THIS? The fact I had such a poor sense of clarity and judgement in this matter was proof of how school had brain damaged me. Thank goodness I had regained my sanity and came here. This place was great!

I could tell Eric was thinking all of the same thoughts as me, as far as how wonderful everything was. Eric and his family (his mom) didn't have any money, so Eric never got to do anything like this, or go anywhere at all. Eric only got to go to the farm camp that time because his mom saved up for an entire year to send him.

Eric was looking around at everything with eyes wide open and a smile on his face. No chores here. No dirt here. No mud. No obnoxious kids for us to be stuck with. This place was going to be nothing but fun!

I think we were both trying to decide what things we would want to do, and which things we wanted to try first. I think we both agreed that time on the beach would be an easy first step. But I saw him eyeing the sailboats, as I had done also. I asked him, "Do you know how to sail a boat?"

Eric replied, "Not really, but I think I could figure it out." Then he asked me, "Have you sailed a boat before?"

I replied, "No, but I would love to learn. It looks like it would be fun."

I think at that point it was agreed that we would be putting the sailboats on our list of things to do. However, we both decided in that moment that what we wanted to do most was eat. We were both starving. Therefore, we decided to go to the office and see Benny so that he could get us all set up with everything, including how we could get food.

We went in to see Benny and he was busy talking to about three staff members at the same thing, but about different issues. It occurred to me how busy Benny must have been ALL OF THE

TIME. He definitely had a full plate of tasks and responsibilities.

We waited for him to be finished, and we told him we were ready for his instructions, and that we were hoping to get something to eat. Benny started into his rehearsed presentation he likely had given hundreds of times before to others. He told us that everything here was for our enjoyment, but that we were responsible for not damaging anything, and that we had to keep him informed of our plans, and ALWAYS had to get prior permission before going off the campus. This meant we would need his permission before taking a hike into the adjacent forest, or before taking a boat off-shore. His rules were very reasonable and somewhat common sense.

Then he asked us, "Did you guys see anything of interest yet?"

I replied, "Yeah, Eric and I are interested in the sailboats."

Benny asked, "Have either of you guys sailed before?"

Eric and I both looked at each other like dumber-and-dumber, and Benny just laughed and said, "I will take that as a no." He continued, "THEREFORE, I will need to show you guys everything about the sailboats before you even touch one, is that clear?"

Eric and I both nodded in compliance. Benny said, "We will schedule a class on how to sail sometime this week when things calm down for me, okay guys?"

We both nodded again in agreement. Then I asked, "Where do we go to eat?"

Benny then reached into his desk drawer and pulled out two cards, and gave one to each of us. He said, "Campers can use the cafeteria restaurant. They serve all kinds of different food, and you can pick out whatever you want, eat whatever you want, and whenever you want. It's open from 7:00AM to 10:00PM. Just show them your card and you are all set."

Eric and I were both staring at our magic cards to happiness, while trying to remember everything Benny was telling us. Benny asked if there was anything else we needed for now, and we could tell he was really busy, so we told him we were all set.

Eric and I went to the cafeteria to eat. The term "cafeteria" might not be kind enough for this establishment. It was not like a school cafeteria with gross food. This place was really great. It had an authentic lodge-style, log cabin type interior, with lots of comfortable tables and chairs. There were counters of food, with everything from meats, burgers, pasta, salad, and desserts. I think the term "wholesome buffet" would have been more appropriate. Eric and I were delighted with it!

We each picked out what we wanted, and settled at a table with a view of the beach. We ate and chatted. Eric at some point even said, "I think I'm in Heaven." Then he said, "Hey, thanks for getting me here."

I replied, "It's no problem. You deserve this opportunity as much as I do." Eric smiled, I think because he thought that was a nice thing to say, but yes, I think he was also remembering the reference to what happened back at the farm. We both just laughed, but left any direct references to the farm unsaid.

Our first night was nice, and we both slept okay. We leisurely dragged ourselves into the cafeteria for breakfast, and decided we would just hang out on the beach all day. So that's what we did that first day. This was literally like being on vacation. Again, I questioned my sanity when remembering how I almost turned all of this down.

Our first several days there were all the same. Breakfast, beach, snacks and drinks from the concessions stands, lots of talks, lots of peaceful silence together, dinner, and bedtime. *Is this what it's like to be an old person on vacation?*

Whatever you want to call it, or however you want to think of it, I was loving this life. I knew we only had a couple weeks currently scheduled, but I was already scheming for a way to extend our stay. I could get used to this!

At some point, Benny found us walking past his office, and yelled to us when he would be available for our sailboat lesson. We took note of the time he gave us, and motioned to him with a thumbs up that we would be there. Eric and I were excited for our sailboat lesson that would take place the next day. Laying on the beach was enjoyable, but we were ready for something new and more adventurous as that point. Careful what you wish for, by the way, because sometimes you get it. But we'll get to that in a bit.

The next day arrived, and we made sure we were at the sailboats on time. Benny was already there getting one of the boats ready to take out. He yelled for us to come over, and that we would get started. Benny had his "coach hat" on, and was giving very direct instructions in a very formal and quick way. Eric and I were focusing and paying attention as closely as we could, hoping not to miss anything.

First, Benny told us rule #1, which was to always wear a lifejacket when on board the sailboat, no matter what, with no exceptions. He even told us that if were going to sit on the boat tied up on shore, he would want to see our lifejackets on. He had made his point.

He showed us where there was an emergency safety kit. He said if we ever got stuck out on the lake, or on-shore somewhere else, we could take out the emergency kit. He showed us what was in it. It had everything a standard medical first aid kit had, but it also had a knife, some of those water-proof wax matches, a flint fire-starter in case the matches didn't work, some twine, and a little flare gun.

He told us that everything we needed to survive a few nights alone was in the kit, but he hoped we would never need it. He then said, "What happens more often than not is that you might get stuck out on the lake with no wind, or for some reason you can't get back to shore. If that happens, go ahead and fire the flare gun, and a lifeguard will go out in a motor boat and tow you back to shore." He added, "That happens all the time."

Then he said, "Now that we have covered the safety issues, let me give you a crash-course on sailing." The three of us climbed on board this medium-sized sailboat that could hold three, but would obviously be more comfortable with only two. He showed us how to string up the sail and all of that. We caught a little wind and slowly started sailing out of the little cove where the boats were moored.

Benny started explaining to us about "tacking," and making a zigzag pattern to catch the wind, in case we needed to sail into the wind. I was beginning to think that this sailing stuff was way more complicated than it originally seemed. I had always envisioned just letting the wind catch your sail, and then you go with it, and just let the sail in or all the way out if you start to tip over. Yes, that was the extent of my sailing knowledge. Laugh if you want.

Of course, I was starting to realize the complications of steering toward destinations when the wind was against you, or coming from an uncooperative direction. I was starting to realize that the wind was difficult and almost always uncooperative. It either wanted to blow you over with force, or it wanted to not blow at all. Then it might change directions, or you would change directions, which would then change everything.

I realized I was fully unqualified to even board a sailboat. As for Eric, he was quietly listening and paying attention. I had hoped this meant that Eric was understanding all of this better than I was. Even though Eric was always quiet and not a people person, I felt he might have been a bit smarter than me. Thus, I was hoping he was figuring all of this out, because I could already see I was not going to be a very good captain.

Benny let us steer the boat a bit, and through sheer good luck and good fortune, things went how they were supposed to go. So, Benny was satisfied that we had a good basic understanding of how to sail, and he was ready to certify us as "sail-worthy," (sort of), as long as we stayed near shore. I knew we had just gotten lucky in passing our little test, and I felt anyone who let us out in a boat would be crazy. But that would not stop us. If someone was silly enough to give us the "keys," we would be going! God help us.

Our lesson with Benny ended, and we recovered from "all of that work" by getting a bite to eat. Despite our self-admissions that we had no idea what we were doing, Eric and I were both excited to try going out in the sailboat alone the next day. It was sort of like when you get your first new bicycle, but you don't know how to ride a bike. You are excited to try it out, but what ends up happening is that you end up with skinned knees and elbows. But you have to learn somehow, right?

The next day came, we had our breakfast, and then went directly to Benny's office. We told Benny that we were going to take a sailboat out. He hesitated, as if contemplating whether or not to actually give us permission. He said, "We have some weather coming in here today, and it won't be a good day to be out there."

I replied, "Yeah, but it's nice out right now."

Benny said, "With sailing, it matters not how it is NOW. It matters more how it WILL BE."

I said, "We will just come back in if it starts to get bad."

Benny nodded his head in understanding and agreement, and said, "If you boys stay right out here fairly close to shore where we can see you easily, and come in when the wind picks up, then I'll let you go out."

Eric and I both nodded in agreement. Benny motioned for us to go on and have at it. So we did. We chose the same sailboat as we had gone out in before because it was most familiar to us. We put on our lifejackets, strung up the sail, and slowly and awkwardly, started to make our way out of the cove.

We were able to get clear of the cove area, and out into the open water. We went out far enough so that no other boats were around us, but Benny and the lifeguards would still be able to see us. We just wanted to relax and talk. We were not looking to test the limits of our sailing skills, because we didn't have any skills.

Eric and I were loving it. There was such a feeling of freedom out there on the open "seas." Yeah, we were only on a lake, but this lake was truly really huge, and it felt more like being out on the sea. You could smell the incredible lake air, feel the sun on you, and breathe in nothing but the zest of what life should be. Being out on the water with the light wind in your face and in your sails at the same time is one of life's greatest joys. I could see why people dreamt of a life out on the seas, sailing endlessly on a sailboat.

Eric and I started to fantasize about sailing around the world one day, and what that might be like. Aside from the fact that we didn't know how to sail, it still seemed like such a wonderful, and even feasible dream, considering we were only teenagers with a dream.

Our fantasy lasted for about an hour before we started to notice the clouds coming in, and the wind picking up. I think we just wanted to continue living in our delusion, so we just ignored the changing weather conditions. However, eventually we couldn't ignore it anymore.

There was one other thing we could not ignore anymore, either. Somehow, gradually, we had drifted, or been blown, much further out into the lake, and quite far from the beach. Our beach now looked more like a speck to us. I suppose Benny could have still spotted us with binoculars (maybe?), but it would be safe to say that we were in violation of his request to stay "close."

I told Eric that we should probably get ourselves much closer to the beach. He agreed, and we attempted to try Benny's tacking methods to get back to where we should be. However, it wasn't working very well. The wind kept shifting, the sail kept flopping from one side to another, and we were too stupid to actually use the sailing methods correctly. If anything, we were drifting farther from shore. I was not one to panic, but I began to see slight panic on Eric's face, and this made me start to panic inside. I had always used Eric as my barometer for whatever situation we found ourselves in. If I could see that Eric was calm, I knew the situation was workable. But if I saw Eric was panicked, I knew I might have a problem on my hands. Well, Eric's expression told me that I might have a problem on my hands.

If that was not bad enough, the clouds and wind were picking up more by the minute. Additionally, there was a fog and mist that had rolled in. *What was going on?* It was a perfectly nice day only a couple of hours ago. Now it seemed that the clouds of doom were surrounding us, and that we were on the cusp of something frightening.

Before we knew it, we were completely swallowed by the fog, a light mist, and the wind was pushing us every which way. We could no longer see where we were, or where we were going. I had gotten the sail and direction fixed so that we were moving at a very fast clip now. But where were we moving to? Were we moving quickly toward shore? Or were we moving quickly further out into the lake? How would we even know? It occurred to me that maybe this is why some sailors bring a compass with them. Of course, we had no compass.

Eric asked me, "Do you know where we are going?"

I answered, "No." Then I added, "But wherever we are going, we are going there quickly." This didn't seem to make Eric feel better.

Then, all of a sudden, the wind picked up very strongly, and at the same time, the rain started coming down upon us. Or should I say we had rain coming AT us. I say it that way, because the rain was going sideways into our faces. We couldn't really see anymore. We had to keep our eyes closed for the most part.

Also, the waves started to get HUGE. In the back of my mind, I had this horrible feeling that we had gone WAY OUT in the middle of the lake for the waves to be that way. My limited knowledge of lakes told me that waves are bigger out in the middle. But then again, it was very windy. I had no idea!! Just guessing.

It was then that Eric and I started discussing what we should be doing. We talked about just taking the sail down and sitting out there, so at least we wouldn't be making it worse by going further out. But the idea of just sitting out there in the pouring rain doing nothing for who knows how long, didn't seem appealing. At least when you are moving in a direction, you feel like you are doing something about your problem. Of course, this is a sign of panic; doing something just for the sake of doing something. The correct answer was likely just stopping.

But we didn't. I think we both were hoping that maybe luck would bring us back home if we kept sailing. It didn't. We were getting pounded by waves that seemed like they were coming from all angles. Meanwhile, the sail was swinging wildly from side to side. There were moments it felt like we might tip over from the sail pushing us over, and other times the waves were washing over into the boat like they were going to sink us. Then all of this would happen from our other side, when the sail would swing over to the other side all of a sudden.

We were screwed. I felt we were in danger. I checked the straps on my lifejacket, and when Eric saw that, he freaked out. I could see the eyes pop out of his head, and then he frantically checked his own lifejacket. Once I saw he was already panicked, I suggested to him what I had already been thinking about for a few minutes. I told him to reach for the emergency kit so that we could have it close by us. I wasn't sure what I was going to do with it, but I felt I needed it near me for some reason.

As soon as Eric started reaching for it, the wind slammed us, pushing the sail to the other direction, and it was tipping the boat over. I was going to just let go of the sail, but then a set of huge waves hit us all at once, and the boat flipped over on its side, so that the sail was then in the water.

Eric was panicking. I knew our situation was dire and had reached "emergency status," but in such situations, I tended not to panic. I was one of those people who worry about all the common things in life, but when something catastrophic happens, I usually remained calm, in a state of focus, or maybe just shock.

I said to Eric, "CAN YOU GET THE EMERGENCY KIT?" He had been closest to it, and had almost grabbed it before we tipped. Eric made an effort to move toward it, but I could see he didn't have it, and he wasn't going to be able to get it. Eric was afraid to let go of what he was holding onto. I could tell he was afraid he was in the water. I never asked him if he could swim, but I started to see that perhaps he was not much of a swimmer, because he had that look of terror on his face that you see on someone's face when they are in water and can't swim.

For a few moments, it looked to me like the sailboat was just going to kind of float sideways. It wasn't sinking. It was just sitting on its side floating. I think it would have kept doing that if it were not for the excessive waves rolling over the sail constantly. The more waves that rolled over on top of the sail, the more the boat was starting to totally tip over.

Eventually, that is what happened. The boat totally rolled over and was upside down. I told Eric to get on top of the boat, which was actually the bottom of the boat. *Perhaps we could just sit on the boat that way?*

Again, I think it would have worked if it were not for the vicious attack of the huge waves every few seconds. It looked to me like the boat was going to sink. I didn't dare tell Eric. He was truly terrified at this point. I really think he felt he was going to die. I had never seen someone that scared before.

I started to process the reality that the boat was likely going to sink. For a millisecond I panicked. But then I remembered that the lifejacket was never going to sink. As long as we had our lifejackets on, we couldn't sink. I started to imagine my lifejacket being this large boat that would keep me afloat. It was like some strange delusion that my mind came up with as a coping mechanism to keep me calm.

Eric figured out what was happening and he screamed, "I'M GOING TO DROWN! I CAN'T SWIM! I'M GOING TO DROWN AND DIE!"

I took a deep breath, and said to him, "ERIC, YOU HAVE YOUR LIFEJACKET! YOU ARE NOT GOING TO DROWN!"

It was then that the boat started to sink. We kept standing on it, as if we were going to ride it to the bottom. But obviously, it just sunk off the bottom of our feet while we stayed afloat.

Eric was crying, but not hysterically. I felt he was keeping himself fairly under control as best he could.

I looked up into the sky. I breathed out. I calmed myself. Then I said in a regular voice, "Eric, come to me." He was only three feet away, and we splashed our way toward each other. I looked at him in the eyes as calmly as I could and said, "Eric, I need you to remain calm, and I am certain we will be okay."

Eric responded, "How do you know this? How do you know we will be okay?"

I said to him, "Because we have on our lifejackets. We have each other. And we are on a lake, not the ocean." I added, "Please calm yourself so that we can make the correct choices."

Eric complied, and we just floated for a couple minutes without any actions or words. I said to him, "See! We can just float like this for hours if we have to. It's fine." I then found the longest loose strap from my lifejacket and I tied it to a strap on Eric's lifejacket. I said to him, "See, you are not going anywhere. We will just float together no matter what happens. Okay?"

Eric nodded his head. He seemed in a much better state now. With him under control, I started to strategize. I went into my state of "logic" that I enter when in such horrible situations. I decided that it was POINTLESS to use even one once of our strength and effort, as long as we could not see anything.

I decided we would just relax and float for now. THEN, the first moment I could see what was around us, we would start swimming toward shore. At that point, we would either eventually reach shore, OR we would be seen by a boat and get rescued. So there! Doable plan! Having this all worked out in my own mind made me feel so much better. I felt I was back in control of the situation.

It wasn't long before Eric asked me, "How long are we gonna float out here?"

I calmly answered, "Until the fog lifts and we can see land."

He seemed satisfied with that answer.

It's hard to say, but I would estimate we floated out there for maybe an hour. It felt like ten hours, but I knew it wasn't because it was still light out. The wind calmed down, the rain stopped, and the fog and mist lifted. There were even some streaks of sunlight finding its way through cracks in the clouds.

I looked around us. I looked in all directions, and I looked very carefully. I recognized NOTHING! I had no idea where we were. None. We could have been on another planet for all I knew. We were totally lost. I accepted that reality without verbalizing it to Eric. Instead, I moved to "plan B." I looked for the nearest land. I saw it. I saw land! I knew in this moment we would survive.

I looked at Eric and said, "You see that land over there?"

He replied, "Yes."

I said, "That's where we are going."

He replied, "Do you know where that is?"

I said, "Yes. It's safety."

He didn't argue with that. But then he said, "Hey, I never told you, but I can't swim. I'm sorry. But there is no way I can swim. I don't know how."

I replied, "Yeah, I figured that out already. You don't need to swim Eric."

He replied, "Then how will we get there?"

I said, "We are already tied together. I am going to swim and pull you with me. BUT your job is to not fight me." I then added, "I need you to pretend like you are going to float on your stomach and paddle with your hands like a dog."

He nodded nervously like he didn't like it, but he was going to comply. I made sure our lifejackets were tied together tight, and I started swimming. Eric was very awkward and clumsy at first, but then he got the hang of it. He felt like extra weight on me for sure, but we were still able to move forward, so it was going to work.

I went at a very calm, relaxed, and steady pace so that I wouldn't wear myself out. I told Eric to also kick his feet, and that helped a little. When he got tired, I told him to just try to float and not act like a dead weight dragging under the water. As long as he stayed mostly toward the surface, I was able to pull him along okay.

As we started to get closer to the land, I realized a bit of disappointing news. The "land" we were swimming toward was only an island. To be honest, I was hoping it would be land, and we could be making a triumphant return to safety and eating burgers ten minutes later. But nope.

I chose not to tell Eric this "news." He would figure it out himself anyways. I knew we still had to go to the island though. Once there, maybe we would be rescued by a boat or something. It was not long before Eric said, "That's just an island."

I replied, "Yeah, but it's safety, and we can rest until we are rescued." He liked my reply.

We finally got to the edge of shore where we could touch ground. We both stood up straight touching bottom. I couldn't feel my body anymore. My arms were more exhausted than I had realized, and my legs were not much better. I don't think I could have gone much further before my body giving out. Eric seemed much more delighted about being able to touch bottom. It was as if the panicked helpless Eric was gone, and the normal, very smart and capable Eric had returned.

I untied our lifejackets so that we could both walk to shore without being six inches from each other. We both stumbled onto land. My legs felt like they weighed a ton, and my arms felt like they were no longer attached to my body. We both settled ourselves onto shore. I think we both needed some moments in our own space, further than six inches apart from each other, and just to gather ourselves together.

Eric gave me a few minutes of peace before asking the inevitable question. He said, "What do we do now?"

I knew this question was coming. I replied, "We wait to be rescued, but we also should walk around this island to see what is on all sides of this island." I added, "I'm looking for more land, except this time not an island." Eric nodded in agreement.

We walked around the perimeter of the island. There was a mixed-bag of good news and bad news. The bad news was that the island was small. I didn't see many good options for building a shelter, and I didn't see a water source other than the lake itself. I also didn't see much for available food sources. If you were going to be stranded on an island, this would not be your first choice. However, the good news was that on the other side of the island, we could see what looked like solid shoreline. It was far away, but close enough to feel reachable.

Eric was also assessing everything in his mind, and he likely knew the best course of action, but he didn't like it, so he didn't mention it. I'm sure he was not interested in getting back into the water again is why. He asked again, "What do we do now?"

I replied, "Nothing. Absolutely nothing. Well, except we need a comfortable place to hang out where we can see any boats that come toward the island."

Eric looked at me, as if he wanted more from me, so I said, "We have to stay here for the night if nobody comes. We are too tired to do anything else today."

Eric got his answer he was looking for. No more movement

today. No more swimming today. He seemed relieved in a way. He started surveying the area to find a good spot that would be comfortable, yet have a great view of the water so that we could spot any boats. We both saw the obvious choice at the same time, and started walking toward it without any words exchanged.

It was pretty crappy for my standards. There was no way to build a real fort with a roof or anything. But it had a nice flat area with some rocks for protection, yet we could still poke our heads up and easily see most of the water surrounding us to check for boats.

I tried to break the tension of despair, and I said, "Where is the nearest burger joint on this island?" Eric laughed and said, "Yeah, my thoughts exactly." I couldn't help myself, and then said to Eric, "That is exactly why we will not be staying on this island." I figured that was a nice and friendly way for me to inform Eric that we were definitely leaving, and possibly swimming again tomorrow.

He looked at me all disappointed and annoyed. I said to him, "Are you hungry, Eric?"

He replied, "Yes."

I replied, "Well there is no food here, so that is why we must leave." I just left it at that, and so did he.

We settled into our little area on the island, and made it as comfortable as we could. I will confess that I was a bit disappointed not to see an entire armada of boats out trying to rescue us. There was nothing. This told me that we must have been VERY FAR from our beach at The Lake.

As it was getting dark, Eric and I were both thinking the same thing. Finally, Eric said it. He quipped, "A fire sure would be nice right about now."

I replied, "Yeah, "the fire" is inside the emergency kit that sunk with the boat."

I think my remark made Eric feel bad because he wasn't able to grab the kit. I didn't mean to make him feel bad. I was just telling it like it was. I sensed this and said, "It's nobody's fault Eric."

We were both really tired. My body was completely exhausted, and I was starting to realize that I had another long swim the next day, AND dragging Eric as well, like we had just done. We both dazed off and fell asleep for the night.

We were awoken in the first light of the early morning by the sound of a helicopter flying off in the distance. I figured they must be looking for us, and I was trying to telepathically get them to fly over closer to us. It didn't work. We saw them flying in the area three different times, but always too far off for them to have any hope of seeing us. I suppose they were searching the open waters looking for the sailboat. Logical. But that was not going to help US any.

Eric and I looked at each other and said at the same time, "I sure am hungry."

I said, "Yeah, we have to leave this island now or we are going die. There is nothing here for us."

Eric knew this discussion of swimming to the shore was coming, and it was like he had prepared an argument for not swimming to it. He said, "How about I stay here on the island and signal for help, and you can swim much faster and easier to the other shore and do the same?"

It was a logical argument. But it was a wrong and horrible argument. I said to him, "I am not leaving you here. I didn't leave you at the creek back at the farm, and I am not leaving you on this island now." I added, "As Frank said, we are only safe when we stay together." I continued, "And as I say, I don't leave anybody behind." "Nobody left behind."

Eric didn't like my rebuttal, but he knew I was right. I just looked at him and said, "Same as before. I will tie your lifejacket to mine, and we will swim together as before."

Eric looked like a kid who was just told to do his chores, even though he already knew he had to do his chores. I said to him, "We are both hungry. We won't eat here. The sooner we go, the sooner we can eat something."

With that, we walked into the water and directly toward the shoreline we had decided to aim for. Eric started paddling and kicking without any debate or protest, and we got on with it. The swimming seemed to go better than before because we had a system worked out that worked fairly well. I tried to stay relaxed and took it slow so that I would not wear out. It was long, but eventually we got there.

When we were able to touch bottom, I untied our lifejackets from each other, and we walked onto shore. My body was aching and numb, both at the same time. We were both checking out where we landed, and it once again came with a mixed-bag of good and bad. The "bad" was that it was very remote, and nobody was around, nor were there any buildings that we could see. We had once again managed to find ourselves in the middle of nowhere.

However, the good news was that it was REAL LAND, and it had lots of trees, shelter options, and I even saw a creek that was running from the forest into the lake. This meant that we likely had a legitimate water source, without having to risk drinking the lake water, which may or may not have been okay to drink.

Eric looked around and saw that rescue would not be imminent, that there was no burger joint on the beach, and he looked at me and said, "NOW WHAT?"

I replied, "We can work with this!" I chanted, "Shelter, Water, Food, Fire." Then I added, "And signaling for rescue after all of that is handled. Those are our missions, Eric." He seemed to like the structure and definitive nature of this situation better than the last one, so he said, "I'll work on a shelter."

I replied, "Perfect." Then I said, "Water is over there. Just drink from where you see ripples, where it is flowing quickly. That will leave us with working on a fire, and then food."

Eric said, "It's going to be interesting making a fire with no matches or fire-making tools."

I replied, "Let's just start by finding some small sticks and dried grass, and set it all on a rock in the sun. We need it to dry out." Eric nodded and went off on his missions.

As far as food, I had two things in mind. I thought I would try to stab fish, or find some little crabs in the water. But I also would remain on the lookout for any kind of fruit or berries that were okay to eat.

I very quickly found a blueberry bush and some sparce raspberry bushes. At least we wouldn't starve to death. But I wanted to do better than that. I made myself a spear. I used a sharp rock to make a sharp point on one end of a good strong stick. Then I looked around for a little cove area that might be shallow for me to walk out into the water, but still have fish that come into it.

I took my new fancy spear and waded out into the water. I was half expecting this to be a "fail," but I was going through the motions anyway, because you never know. Much to my surprise, I saw some small but decent fish swimming in and out of this cove. They looked like "Bluegill fish," or at least that is the name used for them in that area. Sometimes people called them "pan fish" or "sun fish." They are considered a "junk fish," but you could still eat them if you cooked them. You could not eat them raw because they might have worms. But cooked, they are fine.

I patiently waited totally motionless until I saw one come right up to me. It looked like it wanted to nibble on my toes. I took a stab at it, and GOT IT! I couldn't believe it. This was working! I didn't want Eric and I to be scratching over one little fish, so I kept trying for more. I ended up getting two more. I tried for a fourth, but never saw another one. I felt three might be enough for us to be okay, along with the berries I found.

I walked over to where Eric was, and was astonished to see he had built a really big and nice shelter. I had a huge smile on my face, and so did he. I was smiling because I saw his huge and inviting shelter. He was smiling because he saw that I had fish stacked up on the end of my spear. We both said nothing to each other, but gave each other a high-five.

But then the hard part. Fire. I really didn't know how this was going to work. I knew in theory that it would be possible with rocks, but I had never done it before. This is where I was hoping Eric might be a tad smarter and know more about this than I did.

I said to him, "I don't suppose you are an expert at starting fires with rocks, are you?"

He laughed and said, "Not exactly." But then he said, "But I DO know how it works." He then went on to explain that we needed a certain type of rock. I think he said Quartz or something like that. Then he said we needed some metal, or steel specifically. He mentioned that the best way was to hit the right kind of rock onto a knife, or vice versa.

I said, "We don't have a knife. Our knife is in the emergency kit at the bottom of the lake."

We both paused. I thought to myself, and said, "What we need is any kind of steel we can find." I had a thought and started looking at the lifejackets. I noticed our lifejackets had a tiny little metal bracket on the back of them. However, it was small and might be hard to make useful. Also, I was not sure if it was hard metal, or just aluminum. Then I thought that maybe we could get lucky and find a piece of metal laying around somewhere. There is usually junk laying around everywhere on shorelines. Maybe we could find a stray piece of metal laying somewhere. I started looking around.

Sure enough, about a hundred feet down the shore from our shelter, I found an old metal rod. It was really heavy, so I figured it was solid steal. It looked like one of those metal rods that people used to keep different pieces of a dock together.

We got everything together for a fire. Eric found some rocks he wanted to try. We got the dried-out grass that Eric had left sitting on a rock in the sun. Then I looked at Eric and shrugged. I said, "I really have no idea how to do this, or how this works. I need your brilliance." Eric didn't look super confident, but he looked focused on giving it a try.

Eric chose a rock, and started hitting the metal rod with it. It wasn't working. But he kept trying.

He kept moving the rod around, and trying different parts of the rod. He also tried different rocks. He finally found a combination that seemed to want to work. We thought we had seen a tiny spark, so he kept hitting a particular rock against an exact spot on the metal rod. I saw another spark.

I tried to hold the dried grass around that specific area, while I was hoping Eric wouldn't hit my fingers while he kept trying to get more sparks. It took a while, but we kept trying. Finally, just when I felt like giving up, there was a huge spark that flew into the grass. I wasn't sure it was going to ignite. All of a sudden, I saw smoke. I gave it a moment, then blew on it just a tiny bit.

WE GOT FLAME! I dropped it carefully onto a bigger pile of dried grass. We definitely had fire. We quickly put some really dry tiny sticks on it. A moment later, we had a solid blazing fire. WE DID IT! Or should I say, ERIC DID IT.

We were smiling from ear to ear, laughing, and then a high-five. We were starving. Both of us thought the same thing, and wanted to cook the fish immediately. We quickly fashioned marshmallow sticks that we used to cook our fish with. The fish were scaly, and we did not have a filet knife, so we had to just cook the fish, and then kind of break them open and dig out the meat. I never tasted fish so good in my life. Yes, it was probably the worst kind of fish to eat, but to us in that moment, it was the best fish ever. A delicacy!

We each had a fish of our own, then we shared the third one. We had berries for "dessert." Then we had some fresh creek water at a perfect spot that Eric had found, where the water was running quickly over little stones. I knew that in our area of the state, clear creek water running over stones and rapids is usually okay to drink in a pinch. We were certainly in a pinch.

Having enjoyed a nice meal, and having a nice shelter already built, we relaxed a bit while we contemplated our fate. It was starting to get dark, and we both knew we would be spending the night there. It was like we had given up on being rescued. With that said, we were discussing our next strategy for rescuing ourselves.

Eric said, "Should we just walk into the woods and keep walking until we hit a road?"

I thought about it for a moment, and said, "I don't know this area. There might not be any road in those woods. Then what?" I continued, "I think we should just stay here. We have everything we need here. We have shelter, food, and water. We are safe. PLUS, we can see the water, and we only need ONE boat to come through this area, and they will see us." I finished by saying, "We are staying Eric." "And now that we have this fire going, we can't leave and risk not having a fire again."

Eric replied, "Yeah, you are right as usual."

I said to him, "Yeah, and if it was not for you, we would not have this fire, or have had cooked fish." I added, "There was no way I would have figured out the rocks and fire situation without you."

I said, "We are a team." Eric smiled and just stared into the fire as it crackled away and gave us a sense of warmth and comfort.

After some minutes of silence and individual private pondering, Eric said, "Let's ask a question for each of us to answer like we did at the farm campfire."

I replied, "Okay. What's the question?"

Eric asked, "What's your dream? Like, what is your dream of what you want to do with your life?"

I thought for a moment. I wasn't sure, really. I said, "I don't think

I have one grand dream. But if I had to tell you something right now, I would say that my dream is to somehow have the ability to affect people's lives for the better."

Eric responded with, "Yeah but you already do that. I've seen you do it over and over."

I said, "What I mean is that I want to be able to do it on a large scale."

I paused and said, "For example, take what Frank does, and Benny does, and even The Carlisle Trust. Take all of them together and look at what they do for people. Look at what they do for young people like us." I paused and said, "My dream would be to do all of that on a grand scale so I can truly make a big difference in the world." "Maybe if I can do that, my life will have true meaning?"

Eric thought for a moment and said, "Well I think your life already has true meaning. In fact, I think your life has more meaning than anyone our age that I've ever known."

I just shook my head and said, "You are just being nice as usual." Then I laughed.

Before he could say anything else that would make me feel embarrassed or uncomfortable, I asked him, "Now you tell me what YOUR dream is?"

Eric hesitated and said, "You might think this is kind of stupid."

I replied, "No I won't. Your dreams are never stupid. Nobody's dreams are stupid."

Eric said, "Believe it or not, I sort of want to be like Frank."

I said, "How so?"

Eric answered, "Frank has the best of all worlds. Speaking of a life that has meaning, I think Frank has the most meaningful life."

I inquisitively replied, "What makes you say that?"

Eric explained, "Frank lives on a farm where he feels truly connected to nature and to himself. He feels he truly belongs there. Plus, he is living a lifestyle that is very meaningful to him. He takes care of animals, a beautiful farm and property, AND also the kids that stay there."

Eric continued, "Not only does Frank live in such a way that gives him great meaning, but he helps kids create a more meaningful life for themselves."

Eric added, "Frank is pretty much the definition of what is meaningful. And I want my life to be that way also."

I paused and responded to Eric, "What you said is probably the most meaningful dream or goal that I've ever heard."

Eric seemed relieved and happy that I accepted his dream as being valid. Of course, Eric's dream was valid. His dream was not only valid, but it was beautiful. His dream exhibited perfectly the reason why I admired him and considered him my best friend.

I found myself hoping that Eric would realize his dream, more so than my own. Perhaps my dream was partly that Eric would live his dream.

As Eric and I were staring into the fire further contemplating, he suddenly said, "Hey, can I ask you something?"

I replied, "You just did."

He smirked and said, "No, really, I have a serious question."

I responded, "Ask whatever you want."

He thought for a moment and said, "How do you feel so confident, and always keep going, even when things seem scary, full of doom, and even impossible?" He added, "Like when the sailboat was sinking, I thought I was gonna die, but you remained calm and confident like you knew for sure everything was going to be fine."

I thought for a second and said, "I don't know, I've always been that way since I was born." After another moment of thought I said, "I think for me it comes down to a couple things. First, I don't fear things. Well, I fear snakes and bees and heights, but what I mean is that I don't fear big things. I don't fear death. I don't fear things I can't control, like the weather, or what others think of me."

I continued, "I think fear is a person's biggest enemy. Fear paralyzes you, controls you, stops you from taking necessary action, and it causes a person to make bad decisions. If you can set fear aside, you can make clear choices, and do what you have to do, like when the sailboat sunk."

Eric said, "What's the other thing? You said there were a couple things."

I said, "Yeah, the second thing is related, but it has to do with not focusing or complaining about things that you can't control. Most people spend their mental energy on dreading, complaining, or being angry about things they can't control. Instead, I focus on the situation as it has been dealt to me, and accepting that as reality, and then thinking of the options available to me for dealing with it." "It's like how soldiers in war can't focus on people shooting at them. They need to focus on their mission, their training, and making the right choices."

I continued, "I don't spend all my time wishing and hoping things were different. I just focus all my energy on reacting correctly to how things ARE."

I could have rambled on, but I decided to leave it at that. I could tell Eric was taking it all in.

But then I decided to finish my remarks by saying, "I might handle situations okay, but it helps to have someone smarter than me, like you, around. Without you, I would be sitting here freezing my ass off with no fire and no cooked food."

Eric just smiled.

There was plenty more to contemplate, but I was running out of energy to ponder too much more. I could tell Eric was also starting to fade. After another long swim, lots of survival chores, and having had a nice dinner, we were really tired and went to sleep in our fabulous shelter. I kept waking up on and off all night to make sure we kept the fire going. That was our life-line. The fire must never go out! I made sure it didn't.

Despite having to feed the fire a few times, we were able to get some sleep in Eric's comfortable shelter. We were once again awoken early in the morning, but this time by the sound of a motor boat. I sprang up and out of the shelter, and quickly got myself right to the edge of the shoreline. Eric was right behind me.

I could see someone in a little fishing boat coming toward us. I waved my arms wildly to make sure I got their attention. They raised their arm to indicate they saw me. Eric and I anxiously waited for them to pull up to the shore.

It was an older man I had never seen before. I felt he was not from The Lake, and even thought that maybe he might not know about us. When he pulled up to shore, I said, "Wow, we are glad to see you!"

He paused for a moment, as if he was a bit confused by my remark. He then said, "Well, I saw your fire last night. I live way down the lake here, and I thought it was odd that someone would have a campfire in this section of the lake. Nobody ever camps out here." He continued, "I thought I had better come out here this morning just to check things out. We don't want anyone burning the forest down here."

I said to him, "No, we need help. Our boat sank and we were stuck here."

I could see a major light go off in his head and he said, "ARE YOU THOSE TWO BOYS THAT WENT MISSING FROM THE LAKE???"

Eric and I both said in unison, "YES!!!"

The guy responded, "OH MY GOD! WOW! I saw it on the news and everyone around here is talking about it. They think you are dead! They searched the entire lake for the sailboat and couldn't find it."

I responded, "Yeah, the boat sank, but we are still very much alive." Eric and I looked at each other, because we never considered that this would be such a big deal, and that people would think we were dead. I began to wonder if we were going to be in big trouble, and what kind of problems we had caused.

The man said, "That's quite a shelter and setup you guys have there. You two built that yourself?"

I pointed to Eric and said, "Yeah he built it. He's like a woodsman genius. He also made the fire with no matches or anything."

The man seemed very amused and fascinated. However, the gravity of the situation returned to the forefront of his mind and he said, "I should get you back right away. I think we could just boat over to The Lake from here. I will have enough gas to get you there, but they're gonna have to get me some gas so I can make it back home."

I said, "THAT IS NO PROBLEM. I can make sure you get gas and whatever you need once you get us back. I know Benny who runs the whole thing."

The man said, "Oh yeah, I know Benny. That'll work. Well let's get going. You guys want to grab your stuff?"

I replied, "We have no stuff. Only our lifejackets."

The man responded, "HOLY MOLY! It's amazing you survived all this."

I then said to the man, "Sir, let me just put our fire out first."

He replied, "Oh yeah, good thinking, boy."

Eric and I both walked back over to our shelter and fire. There was an odd unexpected feeling that came over us. It was as if we were hesitant or sad to leave our little camp. There was something very special about our adventure that we were sharing. But now it was over and we had to go back to the real world, and all the drama that we had caused.

I put the fire out, and then I looked at our shelter and said, "Best shelter ever built, Eric."

He smiled and said, "Thanks!"

We gave it all one last look, then we turned away and went to the boat. We both climbed into the man's boat and settled ourselves on the front row seat. The man fired up his motor, backed out of our little cove where I had caught our fish, and we were off toward our "home" beach.

The motor was pretty loud, so there was no talking, but I suspect the three of us were having all kinds of thoughts running through our heads. Mostly, I was becoming worried about what my parents were going to do, or say. I was also worried Benny was going to kill us, or if we had caused problems for him.

The ride took quite a while. I am not sure how long exactly, but it seriously was a long time. I could understand why they never found us. We were not even remotely in the correct area near The Lake Camps. Somehow, we had drifted and sailed in between a bunch of islands, and ended up in a totally different part of the lake. And then when we swam from the island to the shore, it put us even further away. The thought occurred to me that if this man had not seen our fire, we might have been stuck there much longer, because it was not an area they would have thought of checking for us.

Anyway, I was anxious to get all of this over with. I figured we were in trouble, and maybe would even have to go home. But I was ready for whatever faced us. Finally, I could see our destination off in the distance. I pointed it out to Eric, and he nodded.

As we got closer and closer, I could see some activity on the docks. I realized that they likely already saw us through the binoculars. As we got closer, I could see what a huge deal this was, and I became embarrassed and horrified.

I could see a helicopter sitting in a flat area near the beach. I could see police cars. And I could see a bunch of people starting to come down to the docks. I guess it was obvious for the man rescuing us where to pull up to. He just had to go where the mass of people were waiting.

When we got close enough to make out details of people, I waved to everyone. This was probably really stupid. But I just did it naturally without thinking. When we were pulling up to the dock, I could see a mix of reactions. I could see the police and rescuers shaking their heads, like they were annoyed, or relieved, or ummm, yeah, annoyed. Then I could see Benny looked very relieved and highly stressed. Then I could see my mother and Eric's mom together, and they were crying like we were dead.

I remember feeling annoyed in that moment. In my mind, we had an accident, we survived, we got through it, and we were back. I guess I was hoping that maybe there would be no drama, and life could be perfectly normal as it was before we left to go sailing that day. Why all the drama? But I suppose this is the thinking of every kid my age who causes a big stink like this.

Eric and I got out of the boat onto the dock. Our mothers ran up to us and hugged each of us. My mother was bawling. I just let her cry. What could I do? Finally, I said, "Mom, I'm fine."

She managed to squeak out a messy reply of, "We thought you were gone."

I replied, "No mom, we were fine. We were always fine."

Once she calmed down, I looked over at Benny. I knew I needed to face Benny right away. I went over to Benny and said, "I'm sorry, but the sailboat sunk. Then we had to do what we had to do to survive. I'm sorry we were so far off-course and hard to find."

Benny gave me a hug and said, "I'm just glad you boys are safe." Then he added, "I want to speak with you boys after you get cleaned up and comfortable."

I replied, "Yes, Sir."

Then I spotted a "Search & Rescue" team packing their stuff up and leaving. They were headed toward the helicopter parked near the beach. I noticed the helicopter said "Search & Rescue" on it. I guess that was the helicopter we had seen a few times. I also noticed the police chatting amongst themselves and starting to walk toward their cars to leave.

A group of people who were not leaving, was a group dressed in suits talking to Benny. I was a bit worried about this for some reason. I decided to walk over there and see if I could hear what was going on.

I couldn't make out everything, but I could tell they were lecturing Benny about something. Never before had I seen anyone lecture Benny. It was ALWAYS Benny lecturing others. I walked right over there, as if I was a mother bear trying to protect her cubs.

I walked up to everyone and said loudly, "Benny, do you need me for anything else?"

Benny used my interruption as the excuse he needed to divert the lecture he was receiving. Benny said, "These folks are from The Carlisle Trust, and they are quite concerned about what has happened here."

I immediately responded, "Well what has happened here is completely my fault." I continued, "Benny had told us not to go very far off shore, and I wasn't paying attention and accidently drifted too far, and then we got caught in the storm."

I once again said, "This is all my fault, and I take complete responsibility for it."

Then one of the men with The Carlisle Trust said, "It looks like you had some help though. The other boy was with you also."

I replied, "No, I was the one sailing the boat. I was making all the decisions. It's completely my fault, and only my fault. Don't blame Eric. And don't blame Benny for any of this. All of you can blame me."

All of them from The Carlisle Trust just stared at me like they didn't know how to respond to my statement. Benny also remained silent. I think maybe they were all waiting for me to walk away, but for some reason I knew to just remain standing there.

This seemed to cause The Carlisle Trust people to give it up for the moment. They told Benny that they could all discuss this another time, and they walked off. I looked at Benny and smiled a bit, because I knew I had done something good for him. Benny, wanting to be very angry with, couldn't hold his stern expression, and he just smiled at me, shook his head and walked off to his office. As he was walking away, he yelled out, "Remember, I want you guys to come see me after you have eaten something."

Since he wasn't even looking at me, I didn't respond. I knew we had to go see him. But first, I had to go back to my mother and get her to go back home. I felt like I was fighting a huge forest fire, and trying to put it out bit by bit.

I returned to my mom, and she said, "Do you think you should come home?"

I replied, "DEFINITELY NOT!"

I think she didn't have the strength to fight me on it, and she just nodded. I could see Eric's mom watching us, as if to see what course of action she should take. I tried to help the situation out by waving Eric over to me, as a way of separating Eric from his mom so that it would be clear to his mom that Eric was staying.

I saw Eric hug his mom and then start walking over to me. My mom saw this and completely gave up on her idea to get me to leave with her. I hugged my mother and told her everything was fine and back to normal. She gave me a tight hug, and walked away.

Finally, Eric and I were alone again. We just looked at each other and gave big sighs. *WHAT A BUNCH OF DRAMA!* I motioned for Eric to follow me back to our lodge. We went into our room, and it was weird seeing everything exactly as we had left it. It seemed like everything that happened was maybe just a dream and didn't actually happen. Yet it did.

We each took a shower and got dressed. Then we headed over to the cafeteria. We walked in, looked at each, and laughed. We both knew exactly what we wanted. BURGERS! We each got two, and some sides. I noticed some people watching us. I suppose they had heard about all the drama. Plus, Eric and I were eating like we had not seen food in many days. Since this was pretty much literally true, we didn't feel bad about eating that way.

When we were done eating, I had this thought to look at Eric, and I said, "I told you we would be fine."

Eric, took a moment, then he said, "I am beginning to think that as long as a person sticks with YOU, things will always be fine." I just laughed.

After a pause I said, "Well, what might not be fine is what happens when we go see Benny."

Eric replied, "Oh yeah," in a dreaded tone.

I said, "Let's just go now and get it over with."

I got up from the table, threw out my trash, and Eric followed. We walked over to Benny's office. Benny was sitting at his desk, like he was just sitting there waiting for us.

Benny looked at us and said, "Are you boys all comfortable and satisfied now?"

Eric said, "Yes, Sir, we are." I nodded in agreement.

Then Benny started in. He said, "Holy shit, young men. In all my years, I have never cursed in front of my students, athletes, or campers, but you two have managed to exceed my limitations for drama, difficultly, and problems." He continued, "I don't even know what to say about all this. I am pissed that you guys didn't listen to me, and you sailed out of the general area of the beach. I am pissed that you sunk my favorite sailboat. And I am pissed that the entire Carlisle Trust organization is all over me."

Then he paused while looking at us and fidgeting with things on his desk.

He then started up again, "But I am completely blown away and impressed with your abilities to survive this incident completely unscathed, like it was just some kind of camping trip for you guys."

He continued, "Marvin, the guy who rescued you, said that you guys had built some kind of fort, and even managed to start a fire with absolutely no fire-starting tools."

When Benny said that, I pointed at Eric. Benny paused then said, "You did that, Eric?" Eric sheepishly said, "Yeah."

I spoke up and said, "Eric built the shelter AND Eric was the one who managed to start the fire with nothing but a rock and an old metal rod." I added, "Eric is nothing short of a survival genius."

Then Eric decided to say something awkward and added, "Yeah, but I can't swim."

Benny looked at him perplexed, and asked, "Then how did you manage to swim all the way to shore?"

Eric pointed to me and responded, "He tied my lifejacket to his, and dragged me all the way to shore while I tried not to sink him." "Then he did all over again the next day when we changed locations."

Benny's eyes popped out a little, there was a tiny smirk on his face, and then he looked at me and said, "So I guess we have a champion swimmer here, and I didn't know it."

I didn't respond to that.

Benny remained silent. He started fidgeting with something on his desk more intensely. It was an excruciatingly long and awkward silence. I looked at Eric by shifting my eyes nearly to the side of my head. He did the same. I was hoping he would get my signal to just remain silent, and not make any sudden movements.

Finally, Benny broke his silence and said, "You guys are going to pay for that sailboat."

Eric and I looked at each other, and I could see Eric was terrified. I looked at Benny and said, "Sir, both of us are penniless. We don't come from money like the other kids here. Our parents could not even afford to send us here."

Benny immediately responded, "I don't want your money. I want you to EARN IT!"

Eric and I looked at each other again. We remained silent. Benny was still thinking.

Then Benny looked at us and said, "I regret to inform you that your little vacation here is over."

Eric and I both gasped with horror. (*Were we being thrown out?*) But before I could say anything, Benny said, "You both now work for me. You are now employees here."

I responded, "What do you mean?"

Benny said, "I am putting you both to work." He then looked down at his desk and pondered some thoughts for a few moments. He looked at me and said, "I am going to train you to be a lifeguard. You will have to pass certification. But then you will work as a lifeguard here looking after the little kids, and everyone else for that matter."

Then he looked at Eric and said, "Since you don't swim, but you are a magician in the forest, I am making you a Junior Camp Explorer. This means you will lead groups of younger kids into the woods and teach them stuff about the forest and survival."

Eric and I both looked at each other and shrugged our shoulders. It all seemed quite reasonable under the circumstances. We then looked at Benny and both said, "Yes, Sir."

Benny said, "Good, you both start tomorrow. Be here at my office at 9:00AM after you have eaten." Eric and I nodded in compliance.

I figured we were done, and I was about to turn around so we could finally escape and walk out, but then Benny started speaking again. He looked at me and said, "I can see why Frank is so enamored with you. You are like a bundle of admirable trouble, bound with brilliance, along with a large dose of teenage recklessness, and yet also adult responsibility at the same time."

I didn't know what to say. I just replied, "Yeah, I don't understand myself either, Sir."

Then Benny seemed to get solemn and serious, and said, "What you did earlier, by taking full responsibility, in front of all of those Carlisle Trust people. Well. That was the biggest dose of courage, strength, and integrity, that I have seen since, uhhh, since, well, since George Carlisle."

He continued, "Frank joked that you reminded him of George, and now I see why. How strange. And how great. Anyway young man, thank you. For what you did."

I didn't dare say anything. It was all too awkward and uncomfortable, even if it was complimentary.

Benny looked at us, and said, "It's both a horror and an honor to have you boys here. But now I need you to pay attention. You will be responsible for looking after young kids. Don't let me down."

He finally stopped speaking and looked like he was ready for us to leave. I looked at him and said, "Yes Sir." Eric followed my lead and said the same. We both walked out of Benny's office.

Eric and I looked at each other and I said, "Well this should be interesting."

Eric replied, "It's okay. We'll get through it together like everything else."

I said, "For sure," and then we put our hands up and gave each other a high-five.

We were ready for our next adventure at The Lake.

CHAPTER TWO

The Mistake

The next morning, Eric and I reported to Benny's office as instructed, and on time. Eric was immediately sent off to meet with the coordinator for the Young Explorers program, whom he would be working for. That left me alone with Benny. He just stood there and looked me over from head to toe. Not sure what he was looking for. I was wearing beach shorts and my favorite t-shirt. I had assumed I would be on the beach, perhaps hanging out in a lifeguard tower, learning the ropes of becoming a lifeguard.

Lord have mercy, I have never been so wrong about something in my life. After looking at me and smirking, Benny went into his closet and was rummaging around for something. He pulled out some shorts and a t-shirt. He threw them at me. I fumbled around to catch them, and barely did so, although very clumsily.

Benny said to me, "This is your new uniform. Wear it with pride. Wear it with respect."

He continued, "If this outfit is not covered with blood, sweat, and tears by the time we are done, then you have not done your job, and I have not done mine. Let's not allow either of those things to happen, shall we, young man?"

He sent me into his restroom to change. I put on my new outfit, which would become my new life. I dare say it might even become my new identity to a degree. But simply, it was only a pair of red athletic shorts, and a white t-shirt that said "Junior Lifeguard" on it. I looked in the mirror at the new me, and I will admit I loved the new look, and I already felt a sense of pride for wearing it.

However, that enthusiasm for my new look was about to be tested, and turned into pain. When I came out of the restroom in my new outfit, Benny led me out of his office and onto the beach.

In my mind, I was thinking he was going to assign me to sit with another lifeguard in a tower somewhere. I was even wondering what type of drink I wanted to get from the concession stand to have with me while sitting in the lifeguard tower for "training." But that was not to be. I clearly had no concept of what training to be a lifeguard was all about.

Down on the beach (with no lifeguard tower near us), Benny pointed out some markers to me. There was the starting line, and the finish line. He told me to run from the start to the finish, and then from the finish back to the start again, without stopping. He took a stopwatch out of his pocket so he could time me.

I just looked at him. I was wondering if he just wanted to test me to see how fast I could do one of these runs. Surely, I just needed to do one of them fast, and then he would see I am fast enough, and we would move on to the next task.

Nope. I did the first set. It was okay. He told me to go

again. Then he told me to do it again. Then he had me do it again. Then I had to do another. And another. And another.

After about fifteen of these sets, I was completely exhausted and out of breath. I asked him, "How many more do I have to do?"

Benny replied, "It's not about how many. THIS is what we are doing today."

I responded in a desperate tone, "You mean I am doing this all day?"

He snipped back, "Yeah, I think so."

In that moment, all of this went from a challenging exercise, to a daunting survival of my existence. I stopped trying to impress him with my speed, and I started pacing myself. Benny even quipped back after a couple sets, saying, "Why are you slowing down, boy?"

I did the best I could. I was running barefoot in the sand, and it was twice as hard as running on a solid surface with sneakers on. It hurt my legs in ways that I didn't think legs could hurt. It was as if there were "regular running muscles," and then there were "running barefoot in the sand muscles." My arms were hurting from trying to compensate for my legs not moving fast enough. My feet were hurting because they were not hitting evenly on the sand. The sand is not flat. My chest was burning, and I was having trouble breathing. My abdomen was starting to cramp, and I figured it was only a matter of time before I puked.

Just when I thought death was near me, Benny would have me stop, take a break, and drink some water. Once I felt I MIGHT be feeling okay again, he would have me do more sets of these sprints.

Right around lunch time, he asked if I wanted to stop for lunch. I just looked at him. I didn't even know what to say. YES, I wanted to stop. But if I ate lunch, I would puke if I had to run more after lunch. He saw me contemplating the predicament, and he laughed. He just said, "Juice and salad, boy."

I nodded my head and walked off to the cafeteria. Who did I see upon entering the cafeteria? I saw Eric sitting alone having lunch. I walked over to him. He took one look at me and said, "Dude, are you okay?"

I replied, "No."

I walked off to go pick out a salad and some juice. I came back to Eric's table and sat down. Eric looked at my meal choice and said, "Good lord, have you turned into a rabbit or something?" I didn't answer, but noticed his huge yummy burger with fries.

He noticed my non-jovial silence to his comment, and he became more serious and said, "How is it going?"

I replied, "I'm going to die."

Eric remained silent, not wanting to say anything else wrong. Once I had some bites of my salad, and some sips of my juice, I felt slightly better. I asked Eric, "How is it going on your end?"

Eric said, "It's really easy. I just have to make sure none of the kids get lost. I basically spend all my time counting kids to make sure I still have the correct number with me on the trails."

Eric added, "The only time it gets difficult is when some kid starts throwing things at other kids, and then I have to break up fights."

I quipped back to him, "So basically you are back at the farm again, babysitting Mark, Alex, and Nathan." We both laughed, and he nodded in confirmation.

I paused and said, "I'm glad it's working out okay for you. But I think Benny is trying to kill me, and I won't make out as lucky as you."

Eric responded, "I know you can do it. You can do anything."

There was something so authentic and genuine about his comment, that it did give me some comfort and confidence. It was a good reminder that I probably could get through this somehow.

When my lunch period was over, I waved to Eric, got up, and left. I went back down to the beach. Benny was there waiting. He looked at me and said, "I was half expecting you to call your mother and run home."

I responded, "I'm not a quitter."

Benny smirked and said, "Yeah, I should have known you aren't." Then he said, "You ready for more?"

I said, "Yes, Sir."

Without him having to ask me, I lined up on the starting line and started in again. Up and back. Up and back. Over and over. This time, I knew he would let me rest every few sets. It was miserable though. My legs started to feel like rubber. I feared I might collapse at some point, but I didn't.

Something inside me wanted to beat Benny at his own game. I had come to realize that maybe he was trying to 'break me.' I wouldn't let that happen. I would stay out there all night if that was what I had to do. I would make him tired of this, and HE would be the one wanting to stop.

Unfortunately, in the late afternoon, my body decided that it wasn't going to cooperate any longer. I finished a set, and all of a sudden had this OVERWHELMING feeling in my abdomen and stomach. I instinctually ran over to the nearest trash can, and I puked. I puked with more force than I had ever puked before. Nothing much came out, but my stomach muscles thought differently. As I was heaving into the trash can, Benny was putting his stopwatch back into his pocket, and he was picking up his water bottle from the ground. By now, I had tears coming from my eyes, but I wasn't really crying. It was just from heaving so intensely. He came over to me and said, "I guess we are done for the day."

Once I stopped heaving, and stuffed my stomach back down my throat to where it was formerly located, I said, "Why are we done now?"

He simply replied, "Because I know when we are done, and we are done."

He started walking away, leaving me at the trash can. But then he turned around and said, "Evenings are when you have your big meals. Eat heavy and whatever you want." He added, "See you here tomorrow morning."

I didn't reply. I stayed near the trash can for a while, making sure I was "done." Then something sort of magical happened. I noticed the sun starting to fade. I looked out onto the lake. I looked down the long stretch of beach. It looked so incredibly beautiful.

In all of my misery, and in all my pain, there was something about all of *this* that I liked. I didn't know what it was, because I was in so much pain, yet there WAS INDEED something I liked. It felt so fully satisfying in a way.

I looked down at my uniform. It was full of sand, dirt, sweat, tears, and even a drop of puke. I remembered what Benny said, and I laughed to myself. I knew I was doing my job, and I guess this meant that Benny was doing his job as well.

That evening, Eric and I had dinner together at the cafeteria, and I had a full satisfying meal. The worst part of this whole deal, besides puking in a trash can, was that Eric and I didn't have any time to hang out anymore. When we got back to our room, I told him I had to go to bed. He totally understood. He was really quiet, and I fell asleep immediately.

When morning came, I was surprisingly ready for my day. EVERY muscle in my body was hurting though. I had trouble getting out of bed and to the bathroom. BUT, my spirits were high, and I felt I could face another day. My body started gradually working after a half hour of limping around our room.

Eric wanted (needed) to go to breakfast, but I felt it would be unwise for me to eat anything. I went with him anyway so that we could sit together at least. He had a full breakfast, and I had some breakfast sausage and juice. I felt that would work okay, and it meant I didn't feel hungry. When we were done, we saluted at each other as a way of wishing each other luck on our days.

I hobbled down to the beach in my uniform, and Benny was there waiting. He looked me over and said, "How are you feeling?"

I replied, "Everything hurts and I can barely move."

He smiled and said, "Good. Progress. And even better that you showed up on time."

I looked at him and said, "Are we doing more sets in the sand today?"

He said, "Nope." He picked up something from the sand and handed it to me. He said, "This is a rescue board. Get used to carrying it. Get used to running with it. You will always have it with you while on duty."

He showed me how to hold it before I took it, and then he suggested I run one set on the beach with the board. I held it as Benny instructed and ran one set. It was more awkward for sure, but Benny seemed satisfied with my performance. He said, "What we are going to do today is practice making a running entry into the water with the board."

He told me he wanted me to start from where we were standing, and sprint down the beach into the water. Once I reached a certain depth in the water, I was to launch deeper into the water with the board, to start swimming. He told me after a few swimming strokes, I could turn around and come back.

I tried what he said. It was not as easy or simple as it sounded. I could understand what he was wanting. He was trying to increase the speed with which I could go from where the water breaks onto the shore, to a point way past that, where I would no longer be able to touch bottom.

I listened to his pointers and tried different things. This exercise was a combination of physical speed mixed with good technique. Once I was better at launching into the water, he had me paddle out a little deeper with the board before turning around and coming back to shore.

Benny was explaining to me that it was all about speed. The faster you can get to the victim, the better chance you have of saving them. He stressed that the lifeguard business was not just about seconds, but half-seconds. He explained how doing a rescue is a long process that can be broken down into steps. First, you need to discover your victim is in trouble, either before they are in trouble, or just seconds after they are in trouble. Then you have to exit the tower quickly, followed by the speed to get to the shoreline. Then you must launch into deep water quickly, followed by paddling to the victim as efficiently as possible. After that, there was a whole bunch of techniques needed in order to "float" the victim, and then bring them back to the shoreline. This entire process needed to be FAST, and it needed to be SEAMLESS.

I could clearly see that he was trying to build my skills, and my speed, in EACH of those steps. And so it went. He had me doing each of those steps separately, and then together. He showed me how to exit from the lifeguard tower, and we practiced different scenarios of me having to run in different directions, at different angles, from tower, through beach, to shore, entering water, and paddling out into the depths.

This went on for days. Benny mixed things up to keep it interesting, and to keep me on my toes. He gave me plenty of rest, and partly, that was intentionally part of the exercises. Sometimes he would tell me to take a break, and then when he saw I had my guard down and relaxed, and he would yell out instructions to do a rescue at a certain point out in the water. I would have to drop my drink or whatever I was doing, and execute the rescue that he had called out.

Eventually, my sore muscles went away, and I noticed I became very fast and efficient at all of the exercises. I had been unwittingly turned into a sprinter and a swimmer. I just hoped he didn't expect me to pursue those sports in school, because I really didn't want to. But in the context of lifeguarding at that particular beach, I was starting to really enjoy it all.

Eric and I had our daily routine of having a quick breakfast, then my pathetic lunch while he had his full lunch, then we would both have a full dinner together. After dinner, Eric knew I would be going to bed early. He started either going out alone, or he would stay in and read quietly.

My lessons with Benny started to get more sophisticated. Next, he would go out into the water with me. I would play the victim, and he would show me different techniques for retrieving a victim, depending on whether they were "fighting the lifeguard," or if they were totally unresponsive/unconscious. I had to learn the responses for many different types of circumstances. He showed me how to float someone on a board, a 'donut,' and other equipment that he brought out. A lot depended on the weight of the victim, and their level of responsiveness, from combative, to unconscious. We practiced them all.

After he had showed me all of the different techniques with me as the victim, we switched roles, and I had to rescue him under different scenarios. He was not a small man, so it was not easy. I realized how much easier it would be to retrieve a small child, rather than a large adult. But I had to be able to do both.

A couple of times he acted like he was trying to attack me and drown me. He pretty much had to show me some "wrestling moves" to deal with such situations. *Had I unwittingly become a wrestler also?*

Once I had all of the basic physical ability, skills, and techniques down, it was time for me to learn the life-saving skills. Everything I had learned up to that point was only to retrieve the victim as quickly as possible. I had not learned anything yet about resuscitating someone, or giving emergency medical treatment.

One morning, Benny had brought down a training dummy with him for me to learn CPR. I had seen this in school before, and had very brief CPR training. But this was going to be very different, and very intensive training.

The dummy was set up so that Benny could put water in its airway. I had to learn how to assess if a victim was breathing, if there was a heartbeat, if they had swallowed water, and so forth. He showed me the importance of clearing the airway before doing anything. Then I would follow steps to determine what course of action would be needed next.

A lifeguard always hopes that expelling water from a victim will be all they need to do. But sometimes CPR would be necessary if the victim was still unresponsive, not breathing, or if there was no pulse. There was a lot to learn. *Now was I a paramedic, as well?* I grew to have a huge respect for the lifeguard profession. It was unbelievable to me the huge range of skills, physical ability, and emergency medical knowledge that lifeguards had to know.

Benny had me go through all the different steps, taking into account all the possible scenarios. I had to do it over, and over, and over again. If I was doing the slightest thing wrong, Benny would yell at me, stop me, and correct me. For example, if my hands were not positioned on the chest EXACTLY correct, Benny would scream, and I would have to start over again. Benny even used himself as a "dummy" at one point so that I could correctly place my hands on a real human chest that was a larger sized adult. And yes, it is different doing this on a person than it is on a training dummy. Benny was clearly expecting PERFECTION with this portion of my training.

After what seemed like forever, training for all of the medical scenarios and techniques, Benny told me that he needed to focus on other things for a few days because he had gotten very far behind on his duties. He set me up to sit with an experienced lifeguard for a few days. Finally, my life became easier.

All I had to do was report to a certain lifeguard tower at certain times, and sit with the other lifeguard. I guessed that Benny was waiting for something to happen so that I could participate in a live rescue with an experienced lifeguard in charge.

It never happened. What I mean is, there was never a need for a rescue. Nothing ever happened. I began to think that maybe lifeguards had to KNOW all of these skills, but in reality, maybe they never used them much, if at all. Even the other lifeguards told me that they almost never had a serious rescue to make. They said usually it was some kid in the shallows who might get a mouthful of water, and a parent would panic and yell for help. But as far as life-threatening rescues, it didn't happen at that beach apparently.

After sitting with some of the lifeguards, and nothing happening, Benny had me meet him at his office. When I went into his office, all he said was, "Congratulations. You worked hard. You earned this," and he handed me a certificate that said I was an official lifeguard at The Lake, and he handed me a new shirt. It was a fresh white t-shirt, but this shirt said "Lifeguard" on it, instead of "Junior Lifeguard."

I smiled and didn't know what to say. Had all of this blood, sweat, and tears (and puke), only resulted in this anti-climactic moment? I was kind of expecting a ceremony, or maybe even a parade, after all I had gone through to earn this. But nope. He has just given me the new shirt, and then looked down at his desk again.

With that said, I will admit I was VERY PROUD of that new shirt that simply said "Lifeguard" on it. Before I left, Benny looked up and made a point of looking at my old red lifeguard shorts and said, "And from now on, your uniform, both shorts and shirt, must be clean and presentable." I nodded and said, "Yes, okay."

Benny told me to report to the office every morning, and my assignments would be posted on the scheduling board, along with all the other lifeguard's assignments. He ended our meeting by saying, "Make sure you pay attention. Always. It's your job to pay attention."

I replied, "Yes, Sir." And with that, I walked out of his office an official lifeguard for The Lake!

My new life as a lifeguard was so much easier than my days of training. I could eat normal meals, had plenty of breaks, and usually only worked half-days. I had plenty of time to hang out with Eric, and I didn't have to go to bed at 8:00PM like a toddler. In fact, Eric's hours were longer than mine. It was usually me who was waiting around for him to get off work.

I remembered that the whole point of me working as a lifeguard was supposed to be a "punishment" for having sunk the sailboat, but to be honest, I loved being a lifeguard. I didn't mind working. I got to sit up in the tower at the beach and relax. Nothing ever happened, and I could just sip my drink and enjoy the sights.

I soon realized another benefit of being a lifeguard. People thought lifeguards were cool. Even better than that, was that girls seemed fixated on lifeguards. If I walked onto the beach in my normal clothes while off-duty, not a single girl would even notice my existence. But if I climbed up into a lifeguard tower wearing my uniform, girls would take notice and stare at me.

Quite often, girls would walk up to the tower giggling, and ask me silly questions as a way of engaging with me. Even though I was normally a shy person, and not particularly interested in chasing girls, whenever I had my "lifeguard face" on, I seemed to have extra confidence, and I liked to show it off and be "the cool guy," even though without my lifeguard uniform on, I wasn't a cool guy at all.

I suppose you could say I became full of myself. This was not natural to me. That is not who I was in my natural habitat. But when you have a bunch of people, such as girls, and others, looking at you, stroking your ego and such, it turns you into a different person sometimes. Perhaps living an entire childhood of being invisible made me love "being someone cool," for a change.

I started paying less attention to my job, and more attention to responding to the girls who would be starting conversations with me below the tower. I would still keep a very close eye on the beach, and would do my regular tasks, but my attention was only 80% on my job instead of 100%. That can sometimes come back and bite you. But a teenager thinks nothing bad will ever happen if it hasn't happened before.

My teenage arrogance was about to catch up with me. I was about to experience a day that I would never forget. It was a day that would forever live in infamy. It seemed like a normal routine nice day at first. I was working a normal shift in one of the towers. Halfway into my shift, there were two girls who came over to my tower. I had seen one of them before, and I knew she kind of liked me. This time she had brought a friend. It was like she wanted to get her friend's opinion of me, or maybe she just wanted to provide entertainment for her friend, by showing how she could flirt with a lifeguard.

Whatever the reason or circumstances, I played right into it. I thought both girls were pretty, so my ego and my hormones were totally interested in engaging with them. As always, I would glance up and down the beach off and on, but then I would try to act cute and cool in my conversations with the girls as well.

We were all laughing about something I had said, when I thought I heard some loud talking off in the distance. I didn't really think much of it at first, because there was always loud talking, yelling, and even screaming, at the beach. Thus, I didn't look over right away to see what it was about. Besides, nothing of great importance ever happened while I was on duty anyway.

After hearing the loud talking, I started hearing some definite yelling. After that, I thought maybe even a scream. In my head, I knew I had to see what it was. I was just going to finish my sentence I was in the middle of with the girls, and then I was going to look over to see what the ruckus was about.

When I finished my sentence, I looked over toward the noises. I saw a group of people gathered on the shore, and I saw a few men running toward my lifeguard tower, and others trying to struggle out into the water off in the distance. I immediately knew something was wrong. I got my binoculars out and looked over toward where the crowd of people had gathered. I thought I saw some little kid in the water, but it didn't look normal. The kid was farther out in the deep part than they should have been, and it looked like there was no movement other than floating.

I felt a shock go through my body, my stomach dropped, and I even thought I almost pissed myself. I instantly calmed and fell into my training. I grabbed my board, exited the tower, and ran to that area of beach at full speed. Without hesitation I launched into the water, and paddled out to where I thought the kid was.

I could hear everyone yelling and screaming. It was very chaotic. It was awful. Even though I was focused on what I was doing, and reaching the kid, I could still hear some of the comments from the crowd on the shoreline. I heard people saying things like, "He wasn't even paying attention," and "Look how long it took him to notice," and things like that. I don't even want to repeat any more of them, because it's too upsetting. I knew I had already screwed up, and I had not even reached the victim yet.

I had to paddle out quite a way. I had no idea how this kid got so far out. When I reached him, I could see it was a young little boy. He was floating in the water with his face downturned. Submerged.

I grabbed him, and I could already see that he looked blue. It was obvious to me and anyone, that he had ingested water and wasn't breathing. He looked dead. He really did. But fortunately, my training was controlling my body, instead of my emotions. My training took over, and I was able to quickly start dragging him back to shore. I went as fast as I could, as if being extra fast would somehow make up for me not seeing him drowning in the first place.

I got him back to the shore very quickly. I already knew he wasn't breathing, and I knew for sure he must have water in him. So without delay or further assessment, I rolled him on his side, but slightly face-down, to see if I could get the water out of him. In my mind, I was running the contingency plans of what I might have to do. I had a dreaded feeling I might have to do CPR on him, and I was nervous because I had never done it before on a real person.

However, when I had him on his side, and trying to get him to expel any water, he all of a sudden puked and started coughing. To be precise, I think I saw water coming out of his mouth first, then he puked, after which he started gasping and coughing.

I kept him on his side so any other liquid could be expelled. I prayed that he would keep breathing and not go unconscious on me again, or worse. There was a huge crowd around me, and some of the women were hysterical and crying. Men were talking loudly about how I never saw him drowning.

The little boy seemed to be in a lot of distress. I could tell that he likely still had liquid in his lungs. He was gasping for air and still not okay. I tried to tune out everything around me, and just focus on the boy. I needed to be sure he kept breathing. I felt I had things under better control though. I knew to keep doing what I was doing, unless he stopped breathing, at which point I would try to give mouth-to-mouth, after checking his airway. I was ready, and I was (finally) on my game.

I knew in the back of my mind that I had already screwed up and failed. I knew this. I knew anything I did at that point would never change the fact that I had already screwed up.

The crowd gathered around me had gotten even larger, as I worked on the boy. I could hear voices in the background saying that people had already called an ambulance. It wasn't long before I heard sirens off in the distance. Other lifeguards had run over to me, but there was nothing left to do. The boy was breathing and just coughing up what little liquid was left in his lungs. He appeared like he was going to be fine.

Still the same, I saw the ambulance had arrived at the parking area, and some of the lifeguards, AND BENNY, were leading the ambulance crew down to where I was. They were carrying their equipment and a stretcher. Once they got to me, they asked me what the situation was. They could see the boy was awake and breathing. I told them the boy had been unconscious and looked blue when I found him floating, but after I helped clear him of fluid, he started breathing on his own.

They asked me how long he was in the water unconscious, and immediately people from the crowd were yelling, "WAY TOO LONG!" I heard a man's booming voice say, "THAT LIFEGUARD JUST SAT THERE AND DID NOTHING, AND LEFT HIM FLOATING IN THE WATER!" I heard the general consensus of the crowd was basically that I was totally horrible and awful, and did nothing, and was useless. Maybe they didn't use those words, but that was the general attitude I was hearing in my mind. It was totally distressing, embarrassing, horrifying, and I just wanted to go into the lake and drown myself.

The paramedic kept looking at me for specific information, but he could also hear the crowd heckling me. Plus, I had no precise answers for him, because I had no idea how long the boy had been floating in the water. The paramedic gave up, and just walked away from me, and they had already started carrying the boy on the stretcher across the beach to the ambulance. This was the first time I saw what I assumed was the boy's mother. She was in a total panic, distressed, and near hysterical. I heard her yelling, "THANK GOD! THANK GOD YOU ARE OKAY!" She was yelling all kinds of other things, but those were the words I heard for sure.

I didn't know what to do next. I was so upset that I couldn't even think. I fell back to my knees on the sand, and started to cry. I just wanted all of those people saying things about me to go away. They seemed to just stand there forever criticizing me to each other.

That's when Benny walked over to me, and said, "Are you okay?" I couldn't really answer him without crying. I just shook my head and kept looking down at the sand.

Then this big man with *that* BOOMING voice walked over to us. He started talking to Benny. I don't even like to remember or repeat what he said. To some degree, I may have blocked it out. But he was saying things like, "WHY DO YOU HIRE IRRESPONSIBLE KIDS TO BE LIFEGUARDS?" "THIS KID JUST SAT IN HIS LIFEGUARD TOWER DOING NOTHING WHEN WE WERE ALL SCREAMING FOR HELP!" "IRRESPONSIBLE RECKLESS KIDS LIKE HIM SHOULD NEVER HAVE RESPONSIBILTY LIKE THIS!"

The man went on and on. Benny just stood there listening to him, saying nothing. What could Benny say? Nothing. The man was correct in everything he was saying. I was a horrible excuse for a human being and didn't deserve to even be there. The man was right. But the man was so MEAN! I will never forget his cutting words, his voice, his attitude. He was one of those awful tough men you could never survive if he were your father. I hated him. But yet, everything he said was correct. So I hated myself also.

Benny just let him go on and on, until the man finally got tired and exhausted all of his hatred for me. The man walked off still muttering insults of how evil I was. By then, the crowd had dispersed. I stayed in the sand, on my knees crying. I was hoping someone would come over and shoot me.

Benny saw how distressed I was and just said, "Come on, let's go back to my office."

I got up and followed him back to his office. He sat me down in one of his chairs in front of his desk, while he took his seat behind the desk. He gave me a moment to further calm down, then he asked, "What happened back there?"

I tried to very calmly tell him the facts. I tried to be as honest and complete as possible. I felt my life was already over, and there was no reason to try and cover anything up, or make myself look better. I just wanted to be honest.

I told him about the girls who started talking to me. I told him I was making conversation with the girls. I told him I heard voices and yelling, and I was just trying to be polite and end my sentence to the girls before looking over at the noise. I told him I looked over to see what was wrong, and I saw what was going on, and immediately ran over. I told him I swam out, got the boy, and brought him back, and so on and so forth. I told him all the facts. I told him how the boy looked dead to me, but I was able to clear his lungs. Then I said, "Thank God he didn't die," and I totally broke down crying at Benny's desk.

I don't know what Benny was doing, or thinking, because I was just looking down at the floor crying. Benny said nothing. Finally, I stopped crying, and was just gasping for air and trying to breathe, I was so upset.

Once I was calmed down, Benny said, "Okay, thank you for being honest and telling me all the details." Then he said, "Why don't you go to your room for the rest of the day, and we will talk again in the morning."

I just nodded and left. I didn't blame him for not wanting to look at me anymore. I wouldn't want to look at me either. I was a disgusting disgrace.

I walked right to my room, threw myself on my bed, and started crying more. I am not sure I had ever been that upset before. I truly wanted to die.

I stayed in that state until Eric got back to the room after his work day ended. I could tell by his face that he had heard what happened. He didn't know what to say. *Maybe he was too disappointed or disgusted in me to say anything?*

But he did finally say something. He said, "I'm really sorry about what happened." I guess he was trying to figure out how to comfort me and he said, "It will be okay. I heard the boy will be fine. I actually heard you saved his life."

I looked at Eric and said, "He almost died. He was DEAD when I grabbed him from the water. He was just floating dead. Completely dead. You didn't see it. And it's all my fault because I didn't see it fast enough."

Eric was listening intently with a compassionate expression, but then he asked, "Why didn't you see it happening sooner?"

I responded, "Because I am an irresponsible worthless loser, and was talking to some girls outside my tower."

I thought I saw a bit of disappointment in Eric's eyes. I think he was expecting a more valid excuse from me. But nope. I had no valid excuse. He didn't ask me anymore questions.

He asked me if I needed any food or something to drink. He offered to go get me anything I wanted and bring it back to the room. I just replied, "I don't deserve anything, and I don't want anything." I added, "But I know you need to eat, so go eat, it's fine."

You could tell Eric didn't want to leave me, but he had just finished working all day, and he was probably starving to death. He had to go eat. He told me he would just get something quickly and be right back.

He wasn't gone long, and when he came back, he brought some snack-type-food that he said was for me if I wanted it. He set it on our table so I could grab it if I wanted.

Then he asked the question that he maybe should not have asked, because it triggered me into making a very harsh decision. He asked, "So what are you going to do?"

For some reason, that question flipped a switch in me, and I flipped out. I responded, "I'M DONE!"

He replied, "What do you mean?"

I said, "I'm done. I'm going home. I'm useless here. It's over. I'm done."

I could tell he was upset by this. I knew he didn't want to be left alone there, and he wouldn't want me to leave. But in that moment, I didn't care.

I think he decided to leave me alone after that, maybe hoping I would calm down. We didn't speak again that night. I eventually passed out and slept.

When I woke up in the morning, I started packing up my things. Eric saw this and was getting very anxious and somewhat upset. He knew how I was though, and he knew that I was going to go through with it. I think he tried to accept I was leaving, but hoping to convince me to come back after a short visit home or something.

I went to call my mom, and told her she needed to come get me. I was expecting all kinds of annoying questions, but there were none. It was obvious someone had already told her what had happened. She agreed to come get me right away.

I went back to my room to speak with Eric before he had to leave for his shift. I told him my mom was on her way. His eyes started to get a little red. I looked at him and said, "I'm sorry I have let you and everyone else down."

I continued, "I would rather die than let YOU down. I wish I could die. I'm sorry I have done this to you. I hope you learn from my mistakes, and I only wish I was half the person that you are. You are truly the one everyone should have their eyes on, not me. I am worthless. YOU are the best person I ever met."

Eric started crying a bit. Then he was trying to choke out some words. After struggling a bit, he said, "I don't care what happened, you are still my hero and always will be."

After that, I was crying also. We cried a bit, I patted him on both shoulders with my hands, then grabbed my suitcase, and I walked out.

I made my way over to Benny's office. Benny was at his desk looking glum. He saw me with my suitcase. He said, "So, you're leaving?"

I replied, "Yeah, I'm useless here. I'm a DANGER here."

He paused and said, "Young man, you made a mistake." He continued, "That should not be the end of the world. You need to learn how to face setbacks in life without melting down to nothing."

I took in what he said. He was right. I nodded and said, "Yeah, I'm not up for the challenge, clearly."

Then he said the words that I would remember and contemplate for a long time. He said, "Don't be a quitter. A person of your potential is not a quitter. When you are ready and willing to live up to your potential, you come back here."

I just nodded, started to get choked up again, and walked out.

I stood in the parking lot waiting for my mother to arrive. I tried not to make eye contact with anyone walking by. I was too ashamed of myself. There was absolutely NOTHING about this entire situation that I was not ashamed of. I think deep down I knew that leaving was wrong, but it was as if I had been sucked into a blackhole of hell, and I was spiraling down to lower and lower depths of pain and bad choices. This entire situation was surely a mistake I would never recover from.

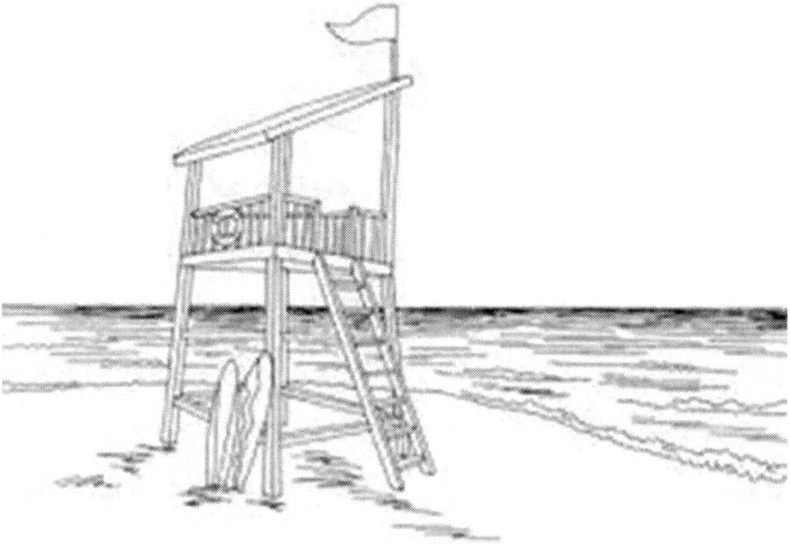

CHAPTER THREE
The Visitations

When I arrived home, I didn't want to see anybody, I didn't want to speak to anybody, and I didn't want anyone speaking to me. I just wanted to be left alone. I was beyond despondent. I was broken. I felt like I had lost myself. I didn't know who I was anymore.

How could I have allowed myself to be so reckless and stupid? How could I have allowed something so horrible to happen? I guess I was not as great as everyone thought. I guess it was only a matter of time before I showed that I was just a loser. Worse than that, I had hurt another person. I had hurt an innocent little boy. Who does that? Who is so incompetent and horrible that they allow an innocent little boy to be hurt and almost die?

Why would anyone trust me with anything again? Anyone would be stupid to even trust me with their dog. I was not worthy to be trusted by anyone for anything. Did I say "dog?" People shouldn't even trust me to get their mail. I would surely drop it in the mud and let it blow away. I was a useless irresponsible dangerous moron.

I honestly could not decide what the worst part was? Was it my guilt over what happened to the boy? Was it that I was angry about being too irresponsible to do my job? Was it that I let everyone else down? Was it that any respect people had for me was completely lost forever? Was it that my life was now over, because surely I had no future anymore?

I was in so much pain from all different directions. I felt I might explode from the inside out, from all of the emotion and intense pain I was feeling. I hated myself. I was so angry with myself. I don't think it was just because I was so stupid and reckless. I think it was because I KNEW BETTER! I WAS BETTER THAN THIS!

I really couldn't cope. I knew Benny was mad at me for leaving. I knew I had let Eric down by leaving. But seriously. I couldn't cope. I couldn't function. Why would anyone want me there, let alone trust me to do anything? I was completely broken. This made me useless in my opinion.

I spent two days up in my room, going from being FUMING ANGRY at myself, to being despondently and inconsolably sad and upset. It was a full meltdown for sure. And the worst part?? Well, it was all so awful, that I couldn't compute what the worst part was. But what came to mind was that IT COULDN'T BE FIXED!

Yeah, I had ultimately saved the kid. He didn't die, thank goodness. My God, can you imagine? I can't even think about it! But besides that, nothing about this situation could be fixed. It happened. It was done. I couldn't have a do-over. Apologizing, working extra hours, or whatever else I could think of, wasn't going to fix this, or make it better. It was one of those things you have to live with for the rest of your life. This was a mistake I would live with forever.

My emotional mood swings and internal outbursts continued for a couple of days. I only left my room to use the bathroom and grab some food to bring up to my room. But once I brought the food up to my room, I found I couldn't eat it. Besides, I didn't deserve food. I deserved to starve and die.

I didn't sleep well either. I would just lay in bed, stare at the ceiling, and continue to have my mood swings of anger and sadness. Eventually, the Universe would have mercy on me and cause me to pass out from exhaustion. I would nap for a few hours, but then wake up, realize my nightmare was still my reality, and I would be off on my internal rants again.

After a couple of days though, I think my mind became numb and broken from it all. I started to feel nothing but hopelessness and depression at that point. I felt dead inside. I was essentially dead. I knew I had no future, no life, no useful purpose, no meaning, no anything. At least the ranting and wild emotional mood swings were gone.

I started to become more philosophical. I found myself looking at the checkers and chess sets that Mr. Wilkens had given me, and wondered how disappointed he would be in me. I wondered what he would possibly say to me at this point. He thought I was so great, but what would my beloved substitute Grandpa think of me now? Would he just dead-bolt his door and never let me in again? Or would he actually have something to say? I wondered.

Another thing I thought about was that speech Frank had given me on my last day of farm camp. I remembered how he told me that I had to step up to the responsibility of being a leader. He talked about how people's lives would depend upon me. At the time, I brushed it off as him being overly dramatic. But now I could see EXACTLY WHAT HE WAS TRYING TO SAY.

It was as if Frank saw the future, and he was trying to warn me that I would have responsibilities that included other people's lives. Frank was ALWAYS RIGHT! How come I was too stupid to not remember what he said, and take my responsibilities more seriously and carefully?

I really didn't know what to do, or what to think anymore. My parents certainly didn't know what to do with me. They never did. But for certain, in this situation, they had no clue. I think they just figured I would either eventually come out of my room and be fine, or I would just die up there. Either way, it would be resolved for them.

I could also see I was not going to resolve this myself. No amount of time sitting on the bench at the park was going calm me or help me resolve this. And I certainly wasn't going to resolve this up in my room alone, ranting, and taking naps.

There was literally only one thing I could think of to do. There was also only one person I felt who could maybe help me. I decided that I should go see Frank at the farm. Yes, I knew he would also be disappointed in me. Yes, he might just tell me to get off of his property because I was so awful. But he was the only one I could think of that might have *SOMETHING* to say, and who I respected enough to listen to and trust.

I had to see Frank. But I didn't want to ask permission first. I couldn't risk Frank or my mother telling me that I couldn't. I was not someone who lied, but I had to get to Frank's without being stopped by anyone. I decided to make a tiny exception to my "always honest" policy, and tell my mother that Frank needed to see me. Come to think of it, THAT might NOT be a lie. Maybe Frank DID need to see me. So, I actually wasn't lying.

So, I went downstairs and told my mom that I had to go see Frank at the farm. She looked at me for a moment like she was about to question me. But then something came over her, and she decided to not ask any questions and just say, "Yes, okay." She asked me when I wanted to go, and I told her as soon as she could. She paused and agreed to take me right away.

I ran upstairs, packed a backpack with just enough stuff for maybe a couple nights, and ran back downstairs. I really wasn't sure if I would be at Frank's for five minutes, or five years. I figured I had enough basics to cover me until I decided what was going to happen. Maybe I could just stay there, and get lost in the woods? Who knows? Regardless, I felt going there was the right thing to do.

I came downstairs with my backpack, and my mom looked at it. She must have figured I was not running away or moving to the farm for long with just a backpack, so she grabbed her car keys and off we went.

We arrived at the farm, and I just had her let me out of the car. I didn't want any weird conversations between my mom and Frank. I just wanted to arrive, her leave, and Frank be stuck with me. I didn't want Frank to say it was a bad time or something, and my mom to not let me stay.

I took my backpack and started looking around for Frank. I knew what time of day it was, and thus I knew what Frank might be doing. He always stuck to a pretty rigid schedule. I was pretty sure he might be milking the cows, so I walked to the cow barn and walked inside.

Sure enough, he had just started milking the cows. At first, he didn't seem to notice me standing there. I wasn't sure what to say, so I just kept standing there silently. Without him even looking up to see me, Frank said, "Why don't you sit down and grab a teat, instead of just standing there like a lost goose."

I honestly didn't know how he knew it was me. Did he have eyes on the side of his head? I set my backpack down and went over to the cow next to him. I knew the routine of how to milk his cows from my time at the farm. But additionally, I had come out to the farm to visit him several times since then, and we would talk while milking the cows. Our routine was to leap-frog each other, so we were always milking a cow next to each other.

I grabbed a clean milk bucket, had a seat, and grabbed a teat as

Frank suggested. I started milking, and still didn't know what to say. Frank let the silence continue quite a while before he said something.

He finally said, "What brings you out here, young man?"

I replied, "I'm here to rot and die in peace."

Frank let a moment pass before replying, "Well that sounds a bit dramatic boy." "And I don't allow anything on this farm to rot without putting it to good use long before that can happen."

I responded, "Then maybe I can just live in one of the barns. I won't be any trouble." Then I added, "Just don't put me in the haunted one on the hill please. It has a skunk."

Frank paused, as if he had just learned something of value that he didn't know, and he said, "That's the first bit of useful information you've given since you've been sitting here boy."

I responded, "Don't worry, maybe the skunk is gone by now."

There was more silence. We both milked two cows before Frank spoke again. He said, "Is this about what happened at The Lake the other day?"

I replied, "Yeah, how did you know about that?"

He responded, "I know most everything that goes on at Carlisle Trust properties."

I kind of froze in that moment because I didn't understand his response, or if he was serious, or joking, or how, or why, he would know what goes on at The Carlisle Trust properties. I knew not to be too nosey and ask, so I just remained silent.

But knowing Frank the way that I did, I knew he was going to remain silent until I said something about what happened. Thus, I said, "I screwed up. I almost let some kid drown, I let everyone down, and I'm a failure as a human."

Without any emotion, Frank replied, "Wow boy, that's quite a resume."

I began to wonder what I was doing there. Frank clearly already knew what had happened, but he didn't have much sympathy or words of wisdom. I was not even sure what I expected from him anyways. Did I expect him to fix this situation somehow? Obviously, he would not be able to. Maybe, I really was there just to rot.

I festered and sulked while I milked another cow. Then Frank said, "So you made a mistake, young man. The question is, what did you do about it afterward?"

I responded, "Well, after I FINALLY got off my ass and saved the boy who was already half dead because of ME, I saved everyone the trouble of dealing with my IDIOTIC INCOMPETENCY, and I left and went home where I could be a useless loser without hurting other people."

Frank replied, "So you quit." "Is that what you are telling me?"

I responded, "Yes, I guess so."

As I knew he would, Frank did not reply, and he let a very long silence go by. We both milked another cow.

Finally, Frank started speaking again. He said, "You know my life-story, young man. I lost everything. I lost my parents, my home, my sense of belonging, everything. I was rejected and moved from place to place, and foster home to foster home. If somebody had reason to lose all hope and give up, it was me. But now I am living my dream and a more meaningful life than I could have ever imagined for myself."

He continued on, "Just imagine if I had just quit and given up long ago when nothing was going right in my life. My life was full of nothing but struggle, hopelessness, and failure. What would have happened if I had just given up and moved into someone's barn to rot and die?"

I knew he would not speak again until he got words out of ME, so I got it over with and said, "You wouldn't have all of this now, and you wouldn't have helped all of us kids that you have helped over the years."

Frank replied, "THAT'S RIGHT!"

This time, I used the inevitable silence to truly process and consider what he had said. Then I said, "Yeah but, how did you endure all of that pain and hopelessness when things seemed hopeless and impossible?"

Frank replied, "I believed in myself. I believed in what was good. I believed in doing the right things." He went on, "I believed that if I kept all of those beliefs long enough, that perhaps something good, or SOMEONE good, would help me change things for myself."

Frank quickly interjected as I was taking a breath to speak, "Notice I said that I intended to change things for myself. I didn't expect anyone to fix everything for me. All I needed was someone, or something, to offer me an opportunity that would allow me to change things and fix things for myself."

I took a moment to consider what he had said. I replied, "Yeah but WHAT, or WHO is going to come along to fix MY situation?

Frank looked at me and said, "You are not listening to me, are you boy?

He went on, "I said nobody is going to fix your situation for you. I said YOU have to fix it. What I said was that eventually there is usually an opportunity, or PERSON, or PEOPLE, who will present you opportunities, or a way, for you to fix your own situation yourself."

I thought again about what he said. I could understand what he was saying, but for the life of me I could not imagine WHAT or WHO, was going to offer me any "opportunity" that was going to fix how I felt about my situation. However, there was no point in arguing. Frank was always right. I just couldn't see how is all.

I think Frank was tiring of my distress, negativity, and doubts, so he said we had talked enough, and that we should eat soon. He told me that I could have one of the guest rooms upstairs in the main house. He suggested I go up, get settled in, and could clean up if I wanted. I think all of this was code for "go away, give me some moments of peace, and chill out please."

I complied, went inside the farmhouse, and went upstairs. I chose the guest room closest to the bathroom, and unpacked the few things that were in my backpack. I laid on the bed for a while, to rest, and to give Frank a rest from me.

However, it wasn't long before he yelled, and called me down for dinner. I sat down at the table and had decided I was going to be mostly silent as to not overly annoy him. I didn't want him to send me back home.

As usual, it was an amazing looking dinner. I looked at Frank, and he looked at me, smiled, and I said, "You. We. All belong here." With that, we started eating. Fortunately for both of us, there were no more complaints or whining from me, and no more lectures from him.

We just made small-talk so that I could get caught up on everything going on at the farm. After we ate, he said he was tired and would be going to bed early. I knew he woke up super early every morning, so it was understandable. I was tired also, since I had not been sleeping well at home.

I went upstairs, decided to take a shower, and then settled into my bed. For some reason, I fell asleep quickly. I slept through the entire night without waking up once. Already, the farm was proving to be good for me.

The next morning, I woke up and went downstairs looking for Frank. He was already outside doing chores (likely since 4:00AM). When I found him, he just looked at me and said, "Rabbit cages." I knew what that meant. I went to where all the rabbits were, grabbed a shovel, and started shoveling out all of the rabbit crap.

It was a disgusting job that I had always hated. But this time, I didn't mind it. As I took each shovel full of crap out of the cages, I imagined that I was shoveling all of the crap out of my head. My head was full of crap. Negative, depressing, CRAP. I shoveled out the crap from my head, shovel-full by shovel-full, while simultaneously shoveling the rabbit crap from their cages.

With each shovel-full, I felt a little bit better. In a weird and twisted way, I was hoping I would never finish. I was wanting more and more rabbit cages full of crap to keep appearing in front of me so that I would never have to stop shoveling. I felt that something cleansing was happening to me, and I needed more, and more, and more.

Unfortunately, I finished all of the cages. Frank came over to check on me because I think he felt I was taking too long. But when he saw all of the cages were not only shoveled out, but almost spit-shined clean, he looked at me in a combination of shock and concern. He said, "I've never seen rabbit cages so clean in my life."

I replied, "Yeah, they were all full of crap, just like me. Needed to be cleaned out." Frank smiled and seemed highly amused and approving of my response.

I looked at him and said, "Next?"

Frank thought, then said, "Chop wood."

I went over to where all of the wood was piled up, and started chopping and stacking it. This work was a bit more physical and difficult, but I was fine with it. Each time I swung the axe and cut a piece of wood, I was thinking of my anger toward myself for my mistakes. Each time I sliced a piece of wood, I was slicing my anger away, one piece at a time, into smaller and smaller pieces.

I did this for hours. I think Frank had peaked over several times to check on me, but he decided not to interrupt, and just let me have at it. I was even surprising myself at how I seemed to be able to chop wood endlessly. I even wondered if I would ever stop, or if I ever wanted to stop. Unlike the rabbit cages, there was pretty much an endless supply of wood to cut. Perhaps I had finally found the perfect never-ending chore for myself to do.

However, eventually Frank came over to me, and handed me a drink. I stopped chopping and took the drink from him, as he was holding one for himself in his other hand also. He motioned for me to have a seat on the stump I had been using as a chopping block. Frank found a good piece of wood for him to use as a seat for himself. We both took some long drinks of our beverages.

Frank said, "Not too long ago when you were here, you were a skinny little guy who would not have been able to swing an axe for more than twenty minutes, let alone many hours. What the hell happened to you?"

I laughed and said, "You can thank Benny for that. Benny spent half the summer turning me into an Olympic sprinter, swimmer, wrestler, weight lifter, jumper, and everything else you can think of." I added, "It was all part of my training to become a lifeguard."

Frank replied, "Well holy crap, it suits you well, young man." He added, "You can work circles around me now. Maybe I should retire."

I quipped back, "No, Sir."

He said, "That's right. And it's not because I am not ready to retire, or that you could not take over everything at this farm. It's because you have other things you need to be doing first." He added, "You have unfinished business to take care of."

I knew he had me trapped and cornered when he said that. I knew there was nothing I could say to respond, so I didn't. He let some silence go by as we finished our drinks. Then he got all serious and said, "I don't mean to be harsh with you young man, but I need more from you."

That really got my attention. NEVER before had Frank said something that I might consider borderline mean or aggressive.

He went on, "Don't get me wrong. I truly think you are amazing. You have already proven yourself to me. More than that, you have proven your character to me in many ways. I truly admire you, and I know you are destined for great things. BUT, I cannot watch you run into a problem, a set-back, or even a failure, and have you just GIVE UP and QUIT." "I can't have it!"

He continued, "I need more from you. I need you to summon the deep character and determination that I KNOW is within you, and I NEED you to stand up like a man, face your challenges, and DO. THE. RIGHT. THINGS."

He kept going, "There are people who are depending on you. WE are ALL depending on you. There are things you don't yet understand, and we need you to BE the person that we all know YOU ARE."

He said, "I am not going to sit here and tell you what to do. You will do whatever you do. But I am here, to remind you now, that you need to live up to your true character, and meet your destiny with the strength, character, and dignity, that we all know you are capable of."

At that point, Frank seemed to make himself stop speaking. It was the first time I ever saw Frank give a lecture that long, and that impassioned. It rocked my foundation a bit. Frank was always a man of wise words, but few words. He never allowed himself to go off on rants. I could tell that this time he was unable to control himself.

I just stayed silent. I had all kinds of thoughts and emotions going on within me. I had never been spoken to like that before in my life. I guess this is what it was like to have a father figure speak to you when you needed it. Every word he said to me was not only correct and accurate, but it was said out of love. I did not take offense. I was not angry, and I was not hurt. I had amassed so much respect for Frank, that I knew every single word he had said to me would be the truth and exactly what I needed to hear.

He was trying to set me straight. I knew he was right. I was not sure I was done sulking or moping yet, but I knew for certain that everything he had said was correct. I also knew that eventually I would have to comply with his terms. I guess I just wanted to do it in my own time. But I knew he was right, and I WOULD COMPLY with his wishes. RESPECT.

But with that said, I did not reply to anything he said, nor did I protest. As for Frank, he was done speaking. 'He had spoken,' and that is all there would be from him for now. I knew this.

It was getting late, and he started heading toward the farmhouse. I knew it was dinner time, so I followed him inside without a word. As usual, he had a dinner delivered from the girl's farmhouse across the road. There were no groups at his farm at the moment, but perhaps the girl's farmhouse had campers who made the dinner.

The two of us sat down at the table, and Frank looked like he was going to just dig-in. I interrupted this and said, "Oh, wait." He looked at me, and I went into a respectful prayer gesture and said, "We all belong here." Frank smiled, and then started digging in, as did I.

We ate mostly without speaking. After we were finished, Frank said, "I have two more things to say to you."

I replied back, "What's that?"

He said, "I want, I need, I would like you, to go see Mrs. Carlisle."

I looked up at him in confusion and shock. Without thinking I said, "Mrs. Carlisle??? Is she even still alive?"

Frank looked back at me like I was being a bit disrespectful in some way. He was right, but I was just shocked by his statement. Last time I had even seen Mrs. Carlisle, I was maybe ten years old. It was about then that she stopped going to the park and sitting on her bench. I guess I thought maybe she had gotten really old, maybe faded away, and maybe passed away? I didn't know. I never gave it much thought. But I also had never heard of any announcements of her passing, so obviously she must have still been alive. I was just being ignorant (again).

Frank said to me, "Mrs. Carlisle is very much alive, and she is much sharper than you or I."

I knew to keep my mouth shut at that point. But there was no way I was going to see Mrs. Carlisle. That was crazy! NOBODY went to see Mrs. Carlisle. She was the Matriarch of our town for as long as anyone in the town had been alive. She was a legend, and it was engrained in every woman, man, and child at birth, that she was not to be disturbed. Nobody even dared knock on her door, let alone speak to her. She didn't know me, nor would she care to know me. This was crazy. But I guess I was going to have to just stay quiet and let Frank speak his piece.

Frank could see I was horrified by his suggestion. All he could say at that point was, "Please just think about it. It is a request from me. You will know what the right thing is to do. I trust you, and I believe in you."

There he went with all of those words of passion again. I hated when he did that, because I had found it impossible to ever defy him, or not fulfill his requests when I knew something meant a lot to him.

After that stunning weighted request, I was not sure I even dared to ask him what else he had to say. However, the curiosity got the better of me. I said, "What was the other thing you needed to tell me?"

Frank calmly said, "I've called your mother, and she is coming out here in the morning to pick you up."

That one kind of hurt a little, but honestly I didn't blame him. I had arrived unannounced, and he let me stay for a few days without complaint. I also knew his feelings about what he wanted from me at this point, and none of those things were going to get done as long as I was at the farm.

I just responded, "Yeah, that's fine."

Frank, wanting to be clear that he was not trying to slight me in any way, said, "I love having you here. You can always come out here anytime you want, son." "But you have business to attend to, and I need you to attend to it."

That made me feel better. And there was something about him using the word "son" that I really liked. It was the first time during this visit that he had referred to me in that way, and I felt it was not just accidentally.

After thinking about it, I felt deep inside that my time there was done also. It was time for me to go back home. I guess I knew this.

We made some small talk after that, and even had some laughs. I left the table and went up to my guest room with a good feeling of gratitude.

Morning came, I showered, packed up my backpack, and went downstairs. Frank was already out doing chores and busy, but he had left breakfast on the table for me. I sat down and ate alone. When I was finished, I went outside.

I took in all of the beauty of the farm and its surroundings. There was something about the place that I always loved. It was a place full of challenges, chores, and hard work, but yet, I still loved everything about the place. I loved being back there, and I would miss it, as I always did.

My problems were not solved. I still had a hollow feeling of despair deep inside me, but I did feel a bit better. The farm had reminded me of LIFE. I was no longer thinking of rotting and dying. I was thinking of life. Frank had given me a lot to contemplate and consider, but I was willing to think about everything now, instead of just shrinking away in a corner waiting to die.

I saw my mom driving up the road and into the driveway. I went to find Frank. I found him in one of the barns, and told him my mom was here, and that I was leaving. He saw that I was about to speak, or give some speech, and he raised his hand to stop me. I just laughed and said, "I just wanted to say thank you."

Then Frank looked like he was going to speak, and I wanted to be funny, so I raised my hand just like he had done to me, and he laughed. Then he just smiled and said, "I just wanted to say that I believe in you."

For a second, I thought I might tear up. But I just gave him a tiny wave, turned around, and walked out. I went over to my mom who was waiting in the car, threw my backpack inside the car, and got in.

My mom didn't say anything at first. She just turned around and pulled out onto the road. Eventually she said, "How was your visit?"

I just replied, "What I needed."

The rest of the car ride was without words. I looked out the window and was thinking of all the things Frank and I had discussed.

We arrived back home and I said, "Thanks Mom," and got out of the car and went up to my bedroom. Other than dinner, I spent the day up in my bedroom thinking. I looked at the chess and checkers set from Mr. Wilkens, and I wondered what Mr. Wilkens would have told me to do at this point in my life. I really wished he was still alive.

However, knowing who Mr. Wilkens really was, I already had my answer. Mr. Wilkens would have had no hesitations about doing what needed to be done, or doing what was expected of him. That's what he had done during his career in military intelligence. I was being silly even wondering what Mr. Wilkens would tell me to do. I knew exactly what he would say.

I thought about everything, and everyone. Benny, Frank, Mr. Wilkens, and my own feelings. It was unanimous, and I knew what I had to do. But I hated it. It was so uncomfortable and awkward, the whole thought of it. But I couldn't deny it. I knew what the right thing was to do. I had to try and go see Mrs. Carlisle.

The next morning, I had a HUGE knot in my stomach. I couldn't believe what I was going to do. I had severe doubts. On its surface it seemed crazy. Nobody bothered Mrs. Carlisle. Plus, she was super old at this point, certainly in her nineties. *Maybe she never even got out of bed anymore?* I was full of questions, doubts, and inhibitions. Even so, I had decided I had to do it. Frank requesting it was reason enough for me to do it, even if it was crazy.

I went downstairs and had some breakfast. My mom was busy doing stuff, but she seemed surprised that I was out of my room and appeared to be dressed up to go out. She asked me, "What are your plans today?"

Without any flinch or emotion, I replied, "Going to see Mrs. Carlisle."

My mom looked like she had just touched an electric fence, and she yelled, "NO YOU WILL NOT!" "Nobody disturbs that lady!"

She saw that I was not reacting and said, "OH, YOU WERE JOKING! DON'T DO THAT TO ME!"

I didn't respond.

She got busy with her various tasks and didn't see me walk out of the house. I started walking toward Mrs. Carlisle's home, which was next to the park. However, the closer I got, the more nervous I became. I also became full of doubts again.

I decided to go sit on the bench at the park first to think about things further. The bench at the park had always been my "safe place," and where I could contemplate things without being disturbed, or without judgement from my mom and stepfather back at the house.

I thought of all the reasons why it was crazy to knock on Mrs. Carlisle's door. Then I thought of the reasons why I should follow through with it. For me, it came down to two paths. Did I want to be a little child that abided by all of the old boring worn out customs of what everyone else did? OR, did I want to become something more, something greater, and live up to my so-called "destiny" that Frank spoke of?

The answer was easy for me. There was something deep within me that told me I was destined for special things. I wanted to take a different path than everyone else. I wanted to do something that mattered. I wanted to live a life that was meaningful to me. There was no way to do this if I did not take risks, and if I did not purposely take the path less traveled.

This would mean doing things that others might consider to be crazy. I knew in my blandness, I still had some "crazy" deep inside, although from where it really came from I had no idea. But I knew it was there.

I convinced myself that it was time to walk the path toward my true destiny. Therefore, I got up and literally started to walk the path that went to Mrs. Carlisle's house. As I was walking, I was reminded of all the times I had, and lessons learned, while at that park. I tried to use those memories as strength for what I was about to do.

Soon enough, I had arrived. I was incredibly nervous walking up to Mrs. Carlisle's door. What was I doing there? What gave me the right to disturb Mrs. Carlisle? The same old mantra kept playing over and over in my mind about how it was an unspoken rule since way before I was born, that nobody would disturb the Carlisle's, let alone knock on the door to their house.

Plus, she was SO OLD! You could say 'ANCIENT.' What was I going to do, talking to an old lady in her nineties? Not only that, but she was a LEGEND. I would not be exaggerating to say that she was considered ROYALTY in our town. I was just some loser teenager who couldn't pay attention and do his job. Let's also not forget that I sunk one of her Trust's sailboats to the bottom of the lake.

The more I thought about it, the more I realized that I was the LAST person that should be bothering Mrs. Carlisle. I should be shot at her front door for the things I did. I was not worthy to pick up dog poo from her front lawn, let alone take up a minute of her time.

I was really beginning to think I should just turn around and go back home. The ONLY thing that stopped me was Frank. I kept thinking that it was Frank who suggested I see her. There is no way I could tell Frank that I didn't do as he asked. NO WAY! Thus, I was going to have to go through with this.

I reached her front steps. I stood in front of her door trembling. I could barely breathe. How would I speak if I can't breathe? It was then that I thought that maybe if I pretended in my mind that she was Mr. Wilkens, that I could calm down and do this. I know that sounds ridiculous.

Mrs. Carlisle was nothing like Mr. Wilkens. Obviously. But I remembered how I was scared of Mr. Wilkens at first also. I also remembered how you can't judge people on the surface. You have to get to know them first.

So, I decided to calm down and pretend I was going to learn more about Mrs. Carlisle, instead of being overly intimidated and terrified. I had to trust Frank.

I knocked on the door, and waited. I didn't want to knock again right away because I didn't want to seem obnoxious or rude. I knew she was old, and maybe it would take her a while to get to the door. Or maybe she was sleeping. Or maybe she was in the bathroom. Or maybe she was eating. Maybe I was disturbing her and she didn't want to answer the door. UGH!

But then the door started to open. I heard some clicking and creaking, and the door started to slowly open. I saw a very frail old woman with a cane. I had trouble in my mind reconciling the grand image of the all-powerful super-wealthy, and legendary Mrs. Carlisle, with the old lady standing at the door in front of me.

She seemed so…old, and so…normal. But I had no reason to doubt she was indeed Mrs. Carlisle, so I said, "Hi ma'am, are you Mrs. Carlisle?"

She looked at me a bit puzzled at first. I don't blame her. I was probably the first person to disturb her at her front door in the last ninety-something years. I guess there is always that ONE moron, and I was him.

I immediately said, "I'm sorry to disturb you. I can go away, or come back another time, or something, if you want ma'am."

She looked at me inquisitively and said in her very elderly but elegant voice, "Deary, why don't you just tell me what you want?"

I replied, "No ma'am, I don't want anything. Umm, I just, umm. Oh, I was here to talk with you, maybe, about something."

She cocked her head a bit and looked at me. I am sure at this point she must have thought I was an imbecile. But then she said, "Are you the boy that Frankie was sending over?"

I said, "Yes. Yes, ma'am."

She then said, "Well why don't you just come inside so that we can talk."

I replied, "Yes ma'am. Thank you, ma'am."

She said, "You can relax Deary, you don't need to be so nervous." She added, "You are so nervous, that you are making ME nervous." Then she laughed.

I replied, "Yes, sorry ma'am. I will try."

She said, "You can call me Bea. It's okay."

I replied, "Yes ma'am."

She started laughing.

It took me a few moments to realize what I had done that was so funny. The thing was, there was NO WAY I was going to call her "Bea." Impossible. She was Mrs. Carlisle to me. Fortunately, she seemed to forgive my inability to comply with her request to call her Bea. I think she just wanted me to calm down a bit, so I did my best to do that.

She led me from the front door, through a hallway, into a sitting area. You could tell this was likely where she held all of her meetings. It was like a living room, but it had no television, and it had an ample amount of seating in the form of couches, loveseats, and those nice upholstered Victorian styled chairs you would find in an old-fashioned traditional parlor.

I couldn't help but let my eyes wander all over the place. I was incredibly curious about her home, perhaps because I had never known anyone who had been inside. On the other hand, her home had a feeling of comfort to me, as if it felt familiar in some way. For some reason, being inside her home caused me to calm down and not be as nervous.

Mrs. Carlisle chose her seat on a very antique, but comfortable looking loveseat. I suppose that is where she always sat. I was not sure where to sit, so I hesitated, hoping for some guidance from her. She waved her hand over to one of those fancy Victorian chairs, which was placed next to where she was sitting, but at an angle so that I could still talk face-to-face with her.

Once I sat down, I placed my sweaty hands onto the arms of the chair, not really knowing what to do with my hands. I sat there like I was waiting for her to say something, even though it was me who had supposedly come to speak to HER. She presumably had no idea why I was there, but so far she was showing very kind hospitality and patience toward me.

A moment later, a middle-aged lady appeared out of nowhere from around the corner and smiled at me. She said, "Would anyone like anything to drink?" I assumed this lady might have been Mrs. Carlisle's caretaker or whatever you want to call it. Mrs. Carlisle looked at me for some kind of answer, and I said, "No ma'am, I'm fine." Then Mrs. Carlisle looked at the lady and said, "Just a little water for me please." The lady slipped out as fast as she arrived, presumably to prepare the drink.

While Mrs. Carlisle was occupied with her assistant organizing her drink, I got a chance to look around at my surroundings. I could see fresh flowers everywhere. I had seen them placed everywhere, from just inside the door, down through the hallway, and now also in the sitting room. I could also see some old black & white photographs in frames that were sparsely scattered about on old antique side tables and display hutches. I could make out a man in most of them, but a man and woman in others. I assumed they were of George, and some of them both together.

Sitting near her, I could catch a slight smell of her perfume. It was very subtle, but it smelled, FELT, very familiar and comforting to me for some reason. I was trying to figure out where I had smelled it before. It was like if Elegance, Class, Wealth, Power, Kindness, and Flowers, all mated, and had a baby. This smell would be that baby. Yeah, I know I sound stupid, but I cannot explain it any other way.

Being inside her home made me feel like I was in a museum of some sort, but at the same time, a very warm and comforting home full of dignity and grace. Basically, Mrs. Carlisle's home reflected *her* in almost every way. I noticed Mrs. Carlisle looking at me, catching me in the act of looking all around. I snapped my attention back to her. Just then, the lady brought in some water in a small glass for Mrs. Carlisle, and sat it down on the end table next to her, after grabbing a coaster for it first. Then the lady swiftly departed, but not before saying, "If you change your mind young man, just give me a holler and I will bring you something." I replied, "Thank you, ma'am."

With that, Mrs. Carlisle looked at me and said, "What can I do for you, Deary?"

I wasn't sure how to start, or what to start with. I started stammering a bit trying to find some footing, and figure out what to say first. I said, "First of all ma'am, I want to apologize for coming to your home and bothering you. I know it is not appropriate for me to be doing this." I continued, "It's just that Frank, or I guess you call him Frankie, well, he is kind of my mentor, and he owns that farm in the country, and I met him at the farm, and well, he suggested that I come see you, and he had known your husband I think, and.."

Mrs. Carlisle started laughing and interrupted me. She said, "Dear, I know who you are. Frankie told me all about you, and he said you might be making a visit."

I replied, "Oh, you know Frank well?"

She laughed again. She said, "Frankie is like a son to me. George knew his father, and George considered Frankie a son for many, many, years." She continued, "Frankie comes to check on me nearly every week, so we have ample opportunity to speak about all kinds of topics, and all of the business matters he helps me with. You, young man, have been a subject of some of those conversations between Frankie and myself."

I just looked at her and did not know what to think of all that. I was confused about how Frank was so deeply involved with Mrs. Carlisle's business matters, and I suppose The Trust. Frank had never revealed this to me, or maybe he had sort of, but again, I was not paying close attention. Plus, was I that much of a problem that they had to discuss me on and off?

I replied, "Ma'am I am very sorry for all the trouble I have caused."

She gave a little laugh, brushed her hand on mine, and said, "No dear, the conversations about you are always very favorable, don't you be concerned." She continued, "Frankie only has good things to say about you. I'm delighted to hear that you consider him a mentor, because Frankie thinks very highly of you, and has a desire to invest much attention in you." She added, "Frankie has told me of your struggles, but never in a negative way, you should know."

I took that as my opportunity to start in. I said to her, "I want you to know how very sorry I am that I made so many mistakes, and I caused so much trouble, and that I have failed all of you in such horrible ways."

Just saying that almost caused me to tear up and maybe start crying. But it also felt good to say it. It was a relief. Mrs. Carlisle just looked into my eyes, with a very kind, soft, compassionate look. She asked, "Why do you feel you have failed us?"

I anxiously replied, "I screwed up. I sunk one of their sailboats. I mean, I guess, one of YOUR sailboats. Or The Lake's sailboats, or whoever or however the situation is. But that was an accident. But it's still my fault."

Before I could say more, she said, "Yes, I know about the sailboat dear. I heard you and another boy went missing and they feared you both might be lost. I am just so grateful that you and the other boy were okay. I am not concerned about the sailboat dear."

I said, "Yes, the other boy was Eric. He's my best friend. None of it was his fault."

She said, "It doesn't matter whose fault it was. It was an accident, and from what I heard, you managed to lead him and yourself to safety against many odds. What Frankie told me happened, and what you did to survive, reminded me of my George, and how he would have acted in the same situation."

Then she said, "If you came here to apologize for the sailboat, please put your mind at rest dear. We have no concern over one lost sailboat. Boats can be replaced."

I decided it was time to jump into what was really most pressing on my mind. I said, "Ma'am, you must have heard about what happened at The Lake with that little boy that I almost let drown." After I said that, I sunk my head, and I was going to start crying. I just kept my head down and tried to get a hold of myself. Mrs. Carlisle remained silent and patient. Realizing she was going to wait indefinitely for me to pull it together and continue speaking, I pulled myself together quickly so I could continue without wasting more of her time.

I looked back up and said, "Benny did his very best to teach me how to be a lifeguard, and I failed him. I also failed everyone at The Lake. I failed The Carlisle Trust. I failed you. I failed the little boy. I failed everyone. After everything people have done for me, I failed everyone."

I couldn't help it, but I was still on the verge of crying, so I stopped and put my head back down again. Mercifully, this time, Mrs. Carlisle wasn't going to remain silent. She said, "I'm so sorry dear." She then put her hand on mine.

She said, "You made a mistake. But you saved the boy's life. I heard the story. You managed to get the boy breathing again."

I responded, "Yeah, but it never should have happened. I wasn't paying attention. I should have seen the boy was drowning and got to him faster."

She then said to me, "Look at me dear." I looked up with my red eyes, but remained silent. She said, "You made a mistake. But you made the best of the situation and still saved the boy. You took full responsibility for your mistake. And I am betting that you have learned a great deal from it all."

I replied, "Yes ma'am, I have. It won't ever happen again."

She said, "Yes, I know this dear. I truly believe you with every bit of my soul."

She paused and then said, "Jonathan and all the great folks who work with The Carlisle Trust told me how you took all of the blame about the sailboat, and the boy in trouble, and didn't want Benny blamed for anything." She gave out a little laugh and said, "They spoke of how you reared up like a wild animal protecting its family. They were afraid to question Benny any further after all you had said in his defense."

I said, "That's because it was not any of Benny's fault. None of it. Benny was the best lifeguard instructor, and the incident with the sailboat was completely my fault as well." I added again, "I'm sorry I failed all of you."

Mrs. Carlisle looked at me square in the eyes and said, "You did not fail us dear. You have never failed us." "You made a mistake. Everyone makes mistakes. Everyone fails at something at certain points. But as long as you do the right thing in the end, you don't fail those who depend on you."

She then paused and seemed to go into a trance as she glanced over to a nearby photo, which I assumed was of George. She said, "Even George failed."

I quipped back, "No ma'am. Everything I heard about Mr. Carlisle was that he was the most amazing man, who did the most amazing things, and he never failed at anything."

Mrs. Carlisle laughed and said, "Deary, George was indeed a great man, and admired by many. But it was not because he was perfect. It was not because he never failed. It was not because he never made mistakes. What made my George a great man was that DESPITE making mistakes, and failing, he always ended up doing the right things in the end."

She paused and looked at me more. Then she said, "I don't know how much Frankie has told you, but very early on in George's career, he had his own business and it failed miserably. We had just gotten married, and we had very little as it was, but we were trying our best to survive and build a life. George got mixed up with a bad bank, and he became over-extended, and he ended up losing everything. His business failed and closed. He couldn't even finish his jobs, or pay his workers anymore. We lost everything."

She stopped; I think to allow me to take it all in. I responded, "How did he start again? I mean, how did he recover from failing like that?"

Mrs. Carlisle replied, "Because of George's integrity and character, there were people who still believed in him, and they helped him start again." She went on, "Because of all the mistakes he had made, he learned a tremendous amount about what to do, and what not to do. It meant that the next time around, he was even better prepared than he would have been without making those mistakes, and without failing."

She said, "Dear, George probably failed and made mistakes as much as anyone, or more so. But he never quit. George was never a quitter."

I could tell that she finished with that thought as a way of wanting me to deeply consider the final statement she had just made.

Her point was not lost upon me. In that moment, I realized that maybe her biggest disappointment, was the fact that I had quit on Benny and The Lake.

She started speaking again, and said, "Everything you see here. Everything you see in this town. Everything you see at The Lake, the high school, and many other places; none of those things would exist today if George had quit after he failed that first time." "George was not a quitter, and that made all the difference in the world, in addition to his great character, of course."

She looked at me, straight into my eyes, and said, "I think you are a lot like George, Deary. You are not a quitter either. In fact, you remind me a lot of my George, with your mannerisms, behaviors, and traits that Frank has described."

She paused. She said, "Frankie says that you were born exactly one day after my George passed away. I find that endlessly fascinating."

She went on to say, "I believe in you, young man, just like I believed in George, and that I believe in Frankie."

Something about her saying that she believed in me, deeply affected me. I thought I might tear up again, but I didn't. I had felt like such a loser and such a failure. It was incredible to me that this lady had the compassion, belief, and willingness, to look beyond my most horrible mistakes, and have such faith in me. Never had anyone in my life risen to that level of faith in me, except for Frank.

I had started to give up on myself, but here were two very important and wise people who STILL had faith in me, even after the greatest failure of my life.

There was something almost spiritual about it. I felt a flame become reignited within me, as a result of her faith in me. It was making me emotional, and very grateful at the same time.

As I was contemplating, she took another close look at me, and she stood up from her couch with her cane. For a moment, I thought she might fall over, and I would have to catch her, but she managed. I asked her, "Do you need help with something?"

She replied, "No, no dear. You stay there. I just need to get something."

I watched her hobble with her cane over to a display table on the other side of the room that had an ornamental chest on it. I saw her open the chest and take something out. She then closed the chest and walked back over to me.

She asked me to stand up so that we were both standing, facing each other. She leaned her cane against her couch and grabbed one of my hands. With her other hand, she revealed to me what she had retrieved from the chest. It was a pinecone. It was a really old, ancient looking pinecone at that.

She offered it to me with her hand, and said, "I want you to have this."

As I took the pinecone from her, she looked deeply into my eyes, like she was going to try and look inside my soul. When I took the pinecone, held it, and studied it closely, I had a flood of emotions fill me from within. I cannot explain it.

I had heard the story of the pinecones from Frank while at the farm. So, I was aware of how Mrs. Carlisle had sent George pinecones while he was at war overseas, as a token of her love. But I still could not understand why I was having such a dramatic emotional reaction to it. Perhaps it was because I knew she was giving me something that I knew was so precious to her?

Whatever the reason, I wept. I couldn't help it. I held the pinecone, staring at it, and wept.

I looked at Mrs. Carlisle, and she was still deeply fixed within my eyes, except this time, she also had tears in her eyes as well. She said, "I knew it," and she started to tear up even more. She held my hand more tightly.

All I could think to say was, "Thank you. This means everything to me."

She composed herself and said, "Let this pinecone remind you of who you are." "Let this pinecone remind you of the faith and belief that we all have in you, dear."

I can't explain it, but I felt different all of a sudden. I felt strong. I felt powerful. I felt determined.

I looked into her eyes and said, "I won't fail you again."

And I meant it. I don't think I ever meant anything as much as I meant that, in the very moment I said it. I think she sensed and felt the feeling behind my words. She smiled and said, "I know you won't. I believe in you. We all believe in you. And we are ALL counting on you, dear."

We broke our grasp of hands, and I somehow knew it was my time to go. I said to her, "I will make things right."

She replied, "I know you will. Like my George, you will always make things right." "That is why we trust you."

I started to walk myself to the door, while she followed. When I got to the door she said, "Dear, if there is anything at all you need, or that we can do, you can count on our full support."

I smiled and said, "Thank you, ma'am."

We gave each other one last look. It was like looking into the eyes of a grandmother, while at the same time seeing a very young woman hidden inside an old lady. It was the deepest bond I had ever formed with someone in such a short time. I left feeling that I had known her my whole life. I left knowing she believed in me. I left knowing that I believed in myself again. I left knowing that I would always strive to do the right things.

I walked out and shut the door behind me. I had the pinecone grasped in my hand, but lightly so that I would not damage it. Since the park was so close to her home, I decided to go sit on the bench at the park before going home.

I reached the bench and sat down. I had just been sitting on this bench a short time ago, broken. Here I was on the bench an hour or so later, a renewed empowered person. I also felt older. I felt that perhaps I had aged several years just in my short time with Mrs. Carlisle.

I no longer cared about my ego. I didn't care to show off to girls just because I was a lifeguard. I didn't care to try and impress anyone. I didn't care about how much authority I might or might not have. I didn't care about how great or awful people might think I was. I only cared now about doing the right things, acting the right way, and honoring the belief and faith that people had put in me.

I sat on the park bench and stared at the pinecone, knowing that very pinecone I was holding, had come from the exact park I was sitting in so many decades, or even a lifetime, ago. I thought about all the history of that pinecone. All of the struggle, the failure, and the incredible success. This pinecone had lived through all of that. If this old pinecone could still be around after all of that, maybe I could also.

I sat for a while, and when I felt I was ready, I stood up and started walking home. I arrived home and went directly up to my room. I found a strong little box to put the pinecone in, and I placed it with the checkers and chess board I had got from Mr. Wilkens.

I started packing. I was going back to The Lake. I should have never left. I was fixing that mistake by going back right away. I put everything back into my suitcase, and was well prepared in a short time.

I walked downstairs with my suitcase and set it by the door. I went to find my mom in the kitchen and I said, "Can you take me back to The Lake please?"

She looked surprised, but pleasantly surprised. She said, "But I thought you wanted to stay home?"

I replied, "No. I am not a quitter, and I belong at The Lake."

She seemed a bit confused and surprised by my sudden change in attitude. She asked, "What changed your mind, son?"

I simply answered, "Mrs. Carlisle."

My mom's mouth swung open, and she dropped the pan she was holding. She started saying, "OH MY GOD, YOU DIDN'T REALLY.." but I cut her off at the pass, and said, "It doesn't matter mom. I just need to go back."

She asked, "When? Tomorrow?

I answered, "No, right now if that's okay."

She looked down at the pan she had just dropped, looked at me, and said, "Okay, let's go."

CHAPTER FOUR

The Redemption

We arrived back at The Lake, and my mom dropped me off. It was early evening, so I decided not to bother Benny until the next morning. Instead, I went right to my room. I opened the door, and Eric was in there looking all sad and lonely reading a book. When he saw me, he sprang up and ran over to give me a hug.

He said, "Dude, I am so glad you are back! It's so boring here without you." He added, "Are you here to stay?"

I replied, "Yep. Staying."

Eric said, "Awesome! Have you told Benny?"

I replied, "Nope, I will save that fun for the morning."

Then he asked, "What made you come back?"

I replied, "Everything." I further explained, "I have lots of unfinished business here, and lots of people counting on me. Plus, I couldn't leave you here to suffer on your own."

Eric laughed, and said, "Everyone's been talking about you and wondering if you would come back. I think everyone thought you would eventually."

I said, "Well, I'm not going to be a quitter."

Eric replied, "If anyone knows you are not a quitter, it's me. I knew that somehow you would make all of this right again. That's one thing I can always depend on you to do."

I replied, "Thanks." "Let's go eat!"

It then occurred to me that Eric had probably already eaten. But he didn't say anything, and if I had asked, he would have lied and said he hadn't eaten, anyways. So, off we went to the cafeteria for a much needed "Lake Burger."

After we ate and went back to our room, we got caught up on what had happened while I was gone. Eric gave me updates on his job as an Explorer Leader. He told me that things were going well, and he enjoyed working with the smaller kids the best. He indicated that they were more receptive to nature, and loved learning new things.

It was funny for me to see Eric talking like an adult, as if he was an elementary school teacher. He seemed genuinely interested in trying to teach the kids about nature and survival. It was as if Eric had aged as much as I had during our brief time apart.

When we were done chatting, he seemed tired, and we both needed to get started early, so we decided to "lights out" as we called it. That was our code phrase for one or both of us needing to sleep. The other could read or whatever, but we turned the light off and the other person would need to remain quiet.

I think he fell asleep right away, but I was awake quite a while thinking about my visit with Mrs. Carlisle. In a way, it was hard to believe it even happened. In some ways it did not seem real, yet I knew it happened. If Mr. Wilkens had been my 'Grandpa,' Mrs. Carlisle had become my new 'Grandma.' Sort of. But she seemed more. Like maybe a friend. Like a mentor! It was like she was an older female version of Frank, or something. I couldn't pin it down, and I just couldn't figure it out, but I knew she was significant to me now.

Anyway, I must have finally fallen asleep, because the next thing I knew, it was light outside, and Eric was up getting ready for his day. I let him get ready first, then I threw on my lifeguard uniform, and we went to breakfast.

Eric wished he could go with me to see Benny, because he wanted to see the look on Benny's face when he saw me again. However, I thought Benny would know I was back already. I was noticing people looking at me and whispering to each other. Obviously, word was likely spreading that I had returned.

After we finished breakfast, Eric took off, and I headed to Benny's office. When I walked in, there were a couple of people in there talking with him, but when they saw me waiting to see Benny, they all scurried out. I waited for them to completely leave the office before I approached Benny's desk.

Benny had a sort of blank look on his face. He said, "What are you doing here, young man?"

I replied, "I'm here reporting for work."

He responded, "I thought you quit."

I replied, "No. I'm not a quitter."

I finally got a slight smile out of him. He paused, was contemplating, looking at his desk, then contemplating more. He saw I was wearing my lifeguard uniform and said, "I hope you understand that I need to consult with the folks at The Carlisle Trust before putting you back in a lifeguard tower."

I immediately replied, "Yes, Sir, of course."

Benny said, "Therefore, I don't know what to do with you for a day or two."

I responded, "I can run errands for you, and take care of various tasks you are too busy to do."

He seemed intrigued by that and said, "Well actually that might be helpful. I've been having trouble keeping up with all of the supplies that the restaurants and concession stands need. Maybe you can help with that."

I said, "Yes, Sir."

So that's what I did. Benny gave me a list of issues he was having, or missing supplies requested by some of the restaurants and concession stands. I learned where all of the food and supplies were stored, and I had a list of suppliers to call for inquiries about the items we needed. I started going around to all of our establishments at The Lake and asking them what was missing, or what they needed. They would tell me, I would make a list, and then I would look for the stuff in our food storage and supply facility. If I couldn't find what was needed, I would call the supplier and enquire about it, and place an order if needed. It was pretty simple once I figured out the system, but I could totally see why Benny didn't have the time to do it. It was really time-consuming and fiddly.

Benny seemed to really appreciate the help I was able to give him. However, on the third day of my new job helping him, he said he wanted to talk to me about my lifeguard duties. He said, "I have spoken to The Carlisle Trust about your lifeguard duties."

I replied, "What did they say?"

Benny paused, as if to add some suspense, and he said, "Jonathan from The Carlisle Trust said that I was to allow you any latitude that you may request, and that I was to support you in any way possible."

Benny gave me a look, as if this order from Jonathan came as a lecture to him, and Benny was needing to do as he was told by his bosses. I just shrugged my shoulders. I said, "So what does this mean?"

Benny said, "To me this means a couple of things. First, I guess it means you can do pretty much whatever you want, including going back to lifeguard duty. But secondly, it means that once again you have shown that you somehow have a direct line to the top authorities." He added, "I'm not sure what it is about you kid, or how you do it, but it's fascinating and intriguing."

I just looked at him and shrugged again. I had decided there was no way I was going to go into any details of how I met with Mrs. Carlisle. It was better I kept things as they were. Benny then added, "Maybe next time I need something from The Carlisle Trust, I should just ask you instead."

I shrugged again, and said, "Maybe," then I laughed jokingly.

Benny asked, "So what do you wish to do, Sir?"

I replied, "I wish to go back up in the lifeguard tower, SIR"

He smiled approvingly, and said, "Sounds good to me." He then looked at the scheduling board and told me which tower to go to and when. I gave him a friendly military salute and walked out.

I ended up having lunch with Eric, and then I had lifeguard duty afterwards, for an afternoon shift. When I got back up into the tower, I thought I would be nervous and feel bad in some way. I didn't. I felt fine being back in the tower. The only thing that was VERY DIFFERENT, was that from then on, I would be incredibly attentive.

There could have been a dozen naked girls screaming my name under my tower, and I would have not given them an ounce of attention. I was all about my work. I was always looking, always checking, and always looking again, in all directions. Nobody was more attentive than me. And if anyone did try to talk to me up in the tower, I would politely tell them that I was not allowed to talk with anyone while on-duty.

Yes, I was not any fun anymore. Yes, the girls stopped coming to visit me at the tower. No, they didn't really like me anymore. And guess what? I was finally a professional lifeguard, and I was acting like one.

There were no more incidences involving swimmers after that, but it did not stop me from acting like there might be one at any moment, and I was always totally prepared for one in case it happened. I finally understood that being a lifeguard meant being on your toes, ready for an incident at any moment, while in reality nothing was likely to ever happen. That is why being a lifeguard was a job and not a vacation. Even if nothing happened, you had to be on edge as if something was about to happen at any moment. Being attentive. Being ready. That's the job.

I took my job very seriously. Some would have called me over-vigilant. I had set a routine for myself of how I would scan the water, and then beach. But then if I saw some tiny thing that looked weird, like a floating cup in the water, I would look at it through the binoculars, and scan the entire beach and water with the binoculars while I had them up to my eyes. The over-vigilant part is that I would do this routine even if nobody was on the beach or in the water. I would also do all of these things at regular time intervals. If the beach was crowded, I might do it every two minutes, and if the beach was empty, then maybe every seven minutes. It might sound insane, and perhaps some of it was illogical, but it gave me comfort to just stick with a routine that I knew had very little room for error, or chance of me missing something.

On one particular morning, I had the first shift of the day. The beach was totally empty, and nobody was in the water. It was common for the beach to be empty in the morning, but we still had to staff every other tower, because sometimes there might be a random crowd of kids that would come early.

I knew it was going to be a boring shift, but I continued my routine of scanning everything with my eyes, and then with the binoculars if something looked weird. As a lifeguard, you learned to "entertain yourself" by looking and watching the slightest things that might be around. For example, there might be two birds fighting on the beach, or maybe one person throwing things into the water. You might break the boredom by watching such little meaningless things if there were no other people, and nothing else to look at.

On that morning, my focal point would be Benny. I spotted him walking from the office, across the beach, and to another lifeguard tower way down from me. Because it was so early, that particular tower was not staffed. Any kids coming to swim always knew to only swim near a staffed tower. Thus, there were no swimmers, or even people, near where Benny was at that tower.

I used the binoculars to try and figure out what Benny was carrying. It looked like he was bringing some equipment to that tower, and I was curious as to what kind of equipment that tower was getting. I couldn't really make it out, but it looked like it was something heavy by the way he was walking and carrying it.

I only watched him for a short time, because enough time had elapsed that it was time for me to do my regular scans of the water and beach in my own area, like I always did. I always made certain I was not distracted by any particular thing for very long, even if the beach was empty.

Therefore, I did my usual scans of my own area close to my tower. When I was finished, I looked back over at the other tower to see what Benny was up to. I couldn't see him. I thought to myself that maybe he had climbed up into the tower when I was doing my other scans, and that he must have been inside the tower.

But then I thought I saw something odd on the beach, at the foot of the stairs that led up into the tower. I assumed it must be some of the equipment he had been carrying. However, it seemed odd, so I did what I ALWAYS did, and I decided to look at it through the binoculars. When I did, I could see that IT WAS BENNY lying on the beach right at the foot of the stairs.

I knew that wasn't right! Without any further thought, I grabbed my rescue board, swiftly exited my tower, and sprinted to Benny as fast as I could run. Yes, I knew I didn't need a rescue board for an issue on the beach, but for a lifeguard, it is instinct and procedure to always grab your board when exiting your tower for any rescue. Anyways, I was able to run to Benny very quickly. When I reached him, he didn't look right. I could tell it wasn't a prank, or a drill, or him just resting.

I assessed the situation, checked his vitals, and I could not detect any pulse or respiration. At that point, I had two strings of thoughts running through my mind. The first was to follow my training and all of the procedures Benny had taught me. The second, concurrently running in the back of my mind, was me wondering what in the world had happened. The only thing I could think of, was that he had maybe had a heart attack while trying to carry the heavy equipment up into the tower.

It didn't matter. At that point, I needed to focus on what I was trained to do. I couldn't believe I was actually doing this, but I was about to start CPR on him. I made sure his airway was clear, lifted his neck slightly as I had been instructed, and gave him a couple of breaths. Then I started chest compressions, putting my hands EXACTLY as Benny had instructed me. It was surreal because when Benny had been training me, he had me place my hands on his chest to show me where they should go. So, I had already had my hands in the exact spot on *his* chest before in training, just as I was having to do now. It felt like I was living some alternative reality nightmare, but I knew it was real, and I had to do exactly what I was trained to do.

Fortunately, the lifeguard in the next tower further down, was on the ball, and he saw through his binoculars what I was doing. He had already been running toward me to assist. When he arrived, I said, "Call an ambulance. Tell them *no vitals*." He immediately took off running. I continued to administer CPR, alternating my breaths and chest compressions, as I was supposed to do while doing CPR alone.

I don't know how long I was doing this for, but it felt like forever.

Realistically, it might have been ten or fifteen minutes. I could finally hear sirens off in the distance. Also, at this time, other lifeguards started running across the beach, because they had been alerted to what was going on by the one who had come over to assist me originally.

A couple of them said, "Do you need to step out?" That was 'lifeguard-talk,' asking if I was getting tired. If I was, I could step out and someone else would take over, or a second lifeguard could assist for two-person CPR."

I replied, "No, I'm good to continue."

It didn't matter anyway, because the ambulance had arrived, and there was a paramedic running at full speed across the beach with his emergency pack. The rest of the paramedic crew was following him a little slower, with a stretcher and even more equipment.

When the first paramedic arrived, I automatically said, "No vitals, maybe fifteen minutes, potential heart attack."

The paramedic said, "I need to shock him then. Continue CPR while I prepare paddles."

I replied, "Affirmative."

It didn't take him long to prepare. He had paddles ready, and by that time the rest of the paramedic crew was standing over us. One of the paramedics standing over me said, "Lifeguard step out."

I did as he said and quickly got up and out of the way immediately. The paramedic crew ascended on Benny as I was getting up, and it was fast and seamless. The paramedic crew proceeded to do what they do best. While a lifeguard might have to deal with this situation on very rare occasion, paramedics often deal with this situation daily. They were incredibly efficient in how they worked as a team. There were very few words between them. They all knew what each other were doing, and what they were going to do.

The only word I heard among them was "CLEAR," and then they shocked Benny with the paddles. They had a specific routine of doing this, then checking vitals, and making sure he got breaths as well. They had to do two rounds of this, and then one of them said, "I have pulse." Right then, we all heard a gasp from Benny, and the other paramedic said, "I have respiration."

I was literally trembling during all of this. I had managed to stay very calm and steady while I was administering CPR, but once I was out of the action, my emotions and adrenaline took over, and I was shaking so much that I thought my legs might collapse. If I had needed to use the restroom before all of this, I would have already peed myself from the adrenaline rush. I had no control over my shaking, or my breathing.

One of the paramedics yelled "STRETCHER!" All of them very quickly and efficiently loaded Benny onto the stretcher. Another paramedic had already run back to the ambulance so they could drive it across the beach right to us. As they were loading him into the ambulance, one of the paramedics asked how long I thought he had been laying there before I discovered him. I told him that I was way over at the other tower, but I doubt it was much more than thirty seconds that Benny was down before I discovered him. The paramedic said, "You were all the way OVER THERE?? And only thirty seconds went by?"

I replied, "Yes, I had been watching him only seconds beforehand."

The paramedic replied, "Nice catch!" Then he resumed focus on his tasks.

Once Benny was all loaded up, the ambulance driver was walking around to get into the vehicle and said, "Nice job lifeguard," as he got into the vehicle. They immediately started driving carefully across the sand to get back into the parking area. At that point, the sirens came back on, and I heard them driving off quickly with sirens blaring, until I couldn't hear them anymore.

Once the ambulance was gone, everyone started coming up to me, asking what happened. People were in shock. It would be a big drama in any circumstance, but because it was Benny, it made for an even bigger drama. Benny was the Director of all operations at The Lake. Everyone knew him, and the entire resort depended upon his leadership. I suppose many thought that the resort would not even be able to operate without Benny.

After a short while, people started walking back to where they had come from, and people stopped asking me what happened. I finally had my first moments alone in peace since all of this started. I was able to get myself calmed down. I still couldn't believe what had just happened, but at least I was not shaking and breathing heavily anymore.

After a couple of minutes gathering myself together again, one of the other lifeguards came up to me and said, "What now?"

I replied to him, "We do our jobs as usual." He nodded in acknowledgement and said, "Let me take over the rest of your shift at your tower so you can take a break." I accepted his offer and thanked him.

Something from within myself made me go straight to Benny's office. I think part of me wanted to connect with him in some way, by being in his office. Another part of me was concerned about his wallet and keys, and I wanted to make sure I knew where they were in case he asked for them at the hospital.

I went into his office and sat down at his desk for just a moment so that I could check for his wallet and see if I could lock it inside his desk, so that I knew where it was, and knew it was safe.

I wasn't sitting at his desk for a minute when a staff worker from the cafeteria came into the office. They clearly had not heard about Benny yet. They first asked if Benny was around, and I just told them "No." Then they went on to explain they were having a problem with running out of a couple of supplies and food items.

Since I had been helping Benny manage the restaurant and concession stand supplies not long ago, I knew what to do in order to check for the supplies. I told the person that I would check on it and fix it for them. I ran over to the supply and food storage area and checked. I could see we had run out. I ran back to Benny's office and found the information to call the supplier. I called the supplier for a delivery as soon as possible.

After I was done with that, I had another one of the lifeguards come into the office. He saw me sitting at Benny's desk and asked, "What are we supposed to do about our schedules?"

I replied, "I can fix the schedules." I had seen how Benny organized and rotated all of the lifeguards, and then put them on the board. I quickly filled in the board for the next day so the other lifeguard could see his schedule. He also asked me what we were going to do with Benny gone. I said the same to him, which was, "We have to keep doing our jobs as normal."

Shortly after him, I had more people coming in, asking questions, and needing things. I answered their questions. When I had a chance, I filled in the rest of the lifeguard schedule board so that people could see their schedule a few days out. I purposely left myself off the schedule, because judging by what was happening with me answering all kinds of questions and solving issues, I was afraid I would not be able to leave Benny's desk to do a regular lifeguard shift.

I lost track of time, and at some point in the evening, Eric came into the office looking for me. He had heard what happened to Benny and was shocked. He said, "Hey, I heard you resuscitated Benny, is that true?"

I replied, "Yes." Then I added, "Well, I did CPR. The paramedics resuscitated him. They had to paddle him."

He looked concerned, maybe wondering if I was really freaked out by the whole thing because of what had happened not long ago with the little boy. However, I was fine. But I WAS hungry. I saw how late it was and said to Eric, "I think it's safe for me to leave now. Can we go eat?"

Eric agreed, and we went to the cafeteria to eat. While we were sitting and eating, I had the staff member who I had spoken to earlier, come to our table and ask me if I had heard anything about the supplies they needed. I informed them that I had placed an order, and that I would check on it for them first thing in the morning. They seemed relieved.

Eric and I finished our meal, and we went to our room. I told him I was really tired and should go to bed early because I was not sure what would happen the next day. He acknowledged and understood. He told me how everyone from all over the resort was really freaked out about Benny, including in his "department," over at the Explorers Camp. I told him to tell me if anyone over there had any major concerns or problems.

I went to bed, and before I knew it, I woke up. It was still dark. My clock said 5:30AM. Normally this meant a lot more time to sleep. But I thought for a moment, and realized that the staff people at the restaurants would be showing up for work at 6:00AM. I needed to check on the supply problems. I got up and made myself ready for work. Eric saw me getting ready so early and asked me if I was okay. I told him I was fine, and that he should keep sleeping until his normal time.

I quickly got myself into Benny's office at 6:00AM. Sure enough, about fifteen minutes later, I had my first restaurant staff member coming in with a problem. By now, everyone knew what had happened to Benny, but they saw me sitting at his desk, and I guess just assumed I was filling in.

Not ONCE did ANYONE ask if I was in charge, or who was in charge. It was a weird accident of timing that I happened to be sitting at Benny's desk the previous day, and everyone automatically assumed that I was the one to speak with about restaurant supply problems and lifeguard scheduling.

I made sure to make careful notes of everyone's problems, and then when I had nobody bothering me for ten minutes, I would make as many phone calls as possible to solve the problems. I had a new appreciation for how busy Benny's job was. I was not sure how he even had time to use the restroom, after what I was experiencing with everyone constantly walking into the office with an issue.

Fortunately, I was able to solve all of the supply issues, one by one. I also made sure all of the lifeguards had shown up for their shifts, and that all of the towers were staffed.

Lunch time came before I knew it. Eric went looking for me and found me in Benny's office again. He reminded me it was time for lunch. I thought for a moment, and wondered if I even dared leave the office for lunch. Then I had a thought, and I asked Eric if he could get our lunch from the cafeteria and bring it back to the office. He agreed that was a good idea, and he went off to get our lunches.

He came back with our lunches and drinks, and we had a good twenty minutes to eat before someone else came in with a problem I had to deal with. When it was time for Eric to go back to work, he left. I asked him to come get me at the office when he was done with work, and we would go have dinner.

Things stayed busy for me. It was late afternoon when I had a different kind of visitor come into the office. It was someone from The Carlisle Trust. I recognized him from that day when we were rescued from the sailboat incident. He was dressed in a suit, looking serious.

Since I already knew he was from The Carlisle Trust, I greeted him very professionally and warmly. I said, "Hello, Sir. How can I help you?" He seemed a bit confused at first. Obviously, he knew me as *that* kid who sunk the sailboat and defended Benny. I am sure he was not expecting to see me in Benny's office, sitting at Benny's desk.

The man said, "I am Jonathan from The Carlisle Trust. I am the Director of Operations."

I stood up and shook his hand, while saying, "Nice to meet you, Sir. I remember you from that day of the sailboat fiasco."

He sort of chuckled and gave me a look, like he was thinking, "*Yeah, no shit you little twerp.*" But he kept his inner comments to himself, and said, "Glad to see you doing well." I replied with a quick, "Thanks."

Jonathan then said, "At The Carlisle Trust main office, we are obviously highly concerned about Benny, and we also need to figure out what is going to happen here with the operations at The Lake while Benny is not here."

He went on, "I wasn't sure if I would be stuck working here, or who was going to handle this place."

Then he asked me, "Who is in charge now? Do you know?"

I hesitated for a moment, and replied, "Nobody is in charge, but I am running everything for the most part."

His eyes popped out of his head and he said, "YOU are running things??"

I replied, "Yes, Sir. Or trying, Sir."

He paused and didn't know what to do with that answer. Then he said, "Well, it looks like the place has not melted-down yet, but I will need to go back to the main office and consult all of our people on how we are going to handle this."

I responded, "Yes, Sir, that's fine."

He took a long look around the office, as if that was going to give him any indication of how things were operating. Then he waved and walked out. I saw him taking more long looks at everything as he was walking back toward the parking area.

I quickly forgot about him, as I had more people with problems walking in my door on a consistent basis. It was early evening, and the shifts had just ended for the outside concession stands. I had a guy named Mickey come into the office. He ran the lemonade stand. He said to me, "Hey, I heard you are in charge while Benny is gone, and I have a problem."

I wondered if I should have told him that I was not actually in charge, but I decided to just remain silent. Instead, I said, "What's your issue?"

Mickey went on to explain that he wasn't making enough money, because he wasn't getting any tips, because his stand wasn't getting much business.

I just stared at him. I was not expecting this to be the kind of issue that I would have to deal with, or that even Benny usually dealt with. I stayed silent and thought for a moment. I knew where his stand was located, and I realized I might know what the problem was. I had an idea! However, I was not ready to share it yet. I told Mickey I had an idea, but I had to do some checking first, and that he should come back to see me in a few days. He agreed.

Eric finally came into the office, and I figured that was my signal to stop for the day and go have dinner. At dinner, Eric told me that in his Explorers department, people didn't know what to do about getting their schedules approved. Without thinking, I replied, "Send them over to the office and I will deal with it."

Eric replied, "Okay, Boss!" We both laughed, and I said, "Don't you even start with that stuff," then we laughed again.

The next morning arrived, and I was back in the office at 6:00AM. Apparently, that was my new work schedule. It was becoming easier though, as I was able to get more on top of the restaurant supply issues. I was able to anticipate some of the issues, and fix them, rather than wait until there was a major immediate emergency.

But there were other issues than just supply issues. I had a familiar visitor pop into the office that morning. It was Eric. He had a pile of papers to give me. He smiled, and said, "Our schedules from Explorer Camp." I smiled back and we both laughed. I said, "Warn them it might take me a day or two." Eric replied, "Yep," and said he had to run back there. We knew we would see each other again at lunch.

However, before lunch, I had an important visitor show up. It was Jonathan from The Carlisle Trust. He came into the office and sat down in one of the chairs in front of my desk. I mean Benny's desk. He looked around again, as if checking to see if anything was on fire or something. Then he looked at me, and said, "Well, I did some checking." Then he went silent.

I said, "Yeah? What did you find?"

He said, "This entire situation we all find ourselves in is a fairly serious issue, plus it's involving Benny, who is a long-time friend of Mrs. Carlisle. So, we presented this entire situation and predicament to Mrs. Carlisle herself." He paused again.

I said, "Yeah? And what have you folks all decided?"

He replied, "Mrs. Carlisle was very specific with me, and said that YOU shall remain in charge of all resort operations here, as long as you are able to handle it."

I think Jonathan was expecting me to be shocked or something. I obviously wasn't. I didn't even blink.

Then Jonathan said, "Mrs. Carlisle has given us very specific direction to assist you, and support you, in any way that you see fit, or request."

Again, not sure if Jonathan expected me to react in any specific way. I did not.

I took a moment, then said, "SIR, I am not in charge. I am only running things until Benny gets back. But I certainly would appreciate any help you can give me."

He seemed to like my response. He asked, "Well. IS THERE anything I can help with??"

I thought for a moment and said, "Yeah. I have a couple of ideas and things I need to take care of."

He looked concerningly perplexed, like he was thinking, "*Oh here we go.*" But all I said was, "I need to have a bunch of signs made. Is that okay?"

He replied, "What kind of signs?"

I said, "I want to put signs up all around the lifeguard towers, and inside, about there being no socializing allowed." I continued, "I was going to ask for this from Benny anyways. It needs to be done."

Jonathan nodded his head in agreement like he thought it was a good idea also.

Then I said, "I am also having problems with the lemonade stand, and I need to get some signage to increase sales there."

Jonathan seemed to think it was a weird request, but nodded with approval.

I said, "With everything having been said, I am going to take care of all the work schedules around The Lake for the other departments also, yes?"

Jonathan said, "Yes, whatever you need to do in order to keep everything running across the resort, you are authorized to do." Then he added, "BUT, because you are under-age, you can't sign any contracts, and I need you to forward them to the main office for us to sign."

I replied, "Yes, Sir, that makes sense."

Then I asked, "Do we know how Benny is?"

Jonathan replied, "Yeah, he is going to be fine, but he won't be back to work for a while."

Jonathan added, "The doctor said that if he had not been discovered as quickly as he was, he would not have made it."

I replied, "Okay, glad he is okay."

Jonathan told me he would check on me next week, and that I should call if I had any problems or needed anything. I thanked him and waved. As he walked out, someone from the restaurant staff walked in. Jonathan hesitated his final exit long enough so that he could see me jump in and handle the next issue being thrown at me. Then he finally exited.

I worked on Eric's schedules for the Explorer Camp so that I could give them to him at dinner, and he could take them to his boss in the morning. I finished, and Eric came in ready for us to go to dinner.

Lucky for me, the entire staff at The Lake had adapted to my schedule. They knew I would be in the office at 6:00AM, but that I would be GONE at dinner time and not be coming back into the office until the next morning. I knew in an emergency they would find me at the cafeteria or in my room within the lodge.

As far as lunch, Eric and I mostly ate in the office, but sometimes we went to the cafeteria. However, staff people would still come up to me while I was eating in the cafeteria, so there really was no difference, and perhaps it was even easier and better to eat in the office.

My daily routine went well, and the days came and went. My mom had heard everything that happened, and she called to ask me if I was ever coming home again. I joked with her that I wasn't. As usual, she didn't think my joke was funny. She reminded me that I had school starting up in the near future. All I could do was roll my eyes and reply, "Obviously. I know."

The day came that my signs arrived. I chased down one of our maintenance guys and explained to him what I wanted done. I had signs that said, "NO SOCIALIZING ALLOWED!" that I wanted installed INSIDE the lifeguard towers. Then I had signs that said, "NO SOCIALIZING WITH LIFEGUARDS PERMITTED" that I wanted installed on the outside of the towers.

I also had signs for the lemonade stand made. They only said, "FRESH LEMONADE," and they had an arrow pointing in a certain direction. So here is the thing about the lemonade stand. The stand was located in a fairly busy area of the beach. However, there were long stretches of beach that always had plenty of people, but there were no drink stands at all. My idea was to install the signs in the areas of the beach that had no drink stands. This way, people who were stuck in the desolate parts of the beach, would see signs for fresh lemonade, and the signs would point them in the direction where they could find the stand. It was an experiment to see if this could increase business at the stand.

It didn't take long to see results from the lemonade signs. Mickey from the lemonade stand came into my office, and excitedly told me how his sales had gone way up, and he was making a ton in tips. He very gratefully thanked me for doing the signs and caring enough to help. I replied to him, "Absolutely. We all appreciate your work here, and I am happy to help you." He left a satisfied "customer."

As far as the lifeguard signs went, nobody said a word. Ironically, I was the reason for them to be installed, so nobody wanted to say anything to me about them. Good.

It wasn't long before Jonathan was back for another visit. He sat down in front of the desk and said, "You seem to have things going pretty well here."

I replied, "Thanks."

He then paused and confessed, "I hope you don't mind, but I checked around with some of the folks here to see how THEY felt things were going."

I replied, "Yeah?"

Jonathan said, "Everyone is saying that you are very responsive to all of their concerns and problems."

I simply responded, "Good."

There was some silence, and Jonathan asked, "Is there anything else you need?"

I responded, "Yep."

Jonathan smiled and almost laughed. I think he knew that might be my answer. He asked, "What do you need?"

I looked at him squarely in the eyes, and said, "I would like defibrillator kits for all of the lifeguard towers." When I said this, I made sure to never break eye contact with him.

There was an air of solemn silence, and there was NO WAY his answer was going to be anything other than "Yes."

He answered, "I will need to get approval for that, but I understand and agree with your request."

I said, "Good. Thank you." Then I added, "I will need someone from the town paramedics squad to come and train all of us on how to use them."

Jonathan nodded his head and said, "Of course."

I could tell Jonathan was afraid to ask me if I needed anything else, but that he was going to ask me that. I stayed silent waiting. He couldn't help himself and indeed asked again, "Is there anything ELSE you need?"

I responded, "Um yes."

He sighed, and said, "Okay, what?"

I said, "You should like this one." I went on to say, "I think I can increase food sales if we put a bunch of picnic tables outside of the cafeteria."

I continued, "I have this idea of having outdoor eating areas with waitstaff service. We can have a very limited menu of just a couple snacks, burgers, and drinks. It will provide more seating, and it will allow us to hire more staff, with that expense being paid for by the increased food sales."

Jonathan looked at me with a very intrigued look. Now I was finally speaking his language. You could tell Jonathan was a "numbers guy." He always sighed when I asked for things that cost money. I was guessing that he probably was in charge of all The Carlisle Trust finances, since he was the Director of all operations.

He thought for a moment and said, "That could work. Let me ponder it first though, okay?"

I replied, "Yeah, sounds good."

There was a silence, and then he looked at me and said, "Hey, I would like to apologize to you."

I replied, "Why?"

He said, "I feel I may have been a bit condescending and dismissive of you at first, maybe because of your age, or the sailboat thing." He went on, "I want you to know that I respect what you have been doing here."

He gave another pause and said, "Mrs. Carlisle used to tell me all kinds of stories about how her husband George conducted business." "What's funny is that how you do things, and deal with people, is similar to how she said her husband George acted."

He added, "You are not bossy like others would be in your position, and you have interesting ideas."

As always happened to me when people started bringing me up in the same sentence as George Carlisle, I was starting to feel uncomfortable, so I just said to him, "That's really nice of you to say. Thank you so much."

Then I said to him, "I don't really know what I am doing. I am just trying to do my best to help out until Benny gets back. But I am very grateful with how you are being with me, and how you are so helpful."

Jonathan smiled, and I smiled, and I figured that would be a good stopping point and signal that he could leave. But before he could step out, I said, "Just let me know on the restaurant idea and the picnic tables please, and I would be very grateful."

He replied, "Yes, Sir."

I immediately replied, "Thank YOU, SIR."

He left and I was thinking to myself, *"Did the DIRECTOR of The Carlisle Trust just call me SIR?"* That moment confirmed for me that I had shed my ego, because instead of feeling like a bigger person, I felt a bit uncomfortable about it. But I knew he was just trying to be nice and show he respected me, which was nice.

It was the following week when I received a message from Jonathan, that Mrs. Carlisle had approved the defibrillators, and they would be delivered, but that I should leave them in the boxes until a training session was set up with the local paramedic squad. He also confirmed that he wanted to work with me, the two of us together, on the "outside restaurant expansion."

However, my time as the leader of The Lake, or whatever you want to call me, was about to end. Benny was out of the hospital, and had been recovering at home. Benny was not a guy you could keep cooped up inside for long, and he was itching to come back to work. I knew I would have to slide out of my position very soon.

One day, Benny finally came to the office. I will admit it was really awkward and uncomfortable for me to be sitting at HIS desk, as if I owned it, when he walked in. I jumped up out of the chair, and removed myself from behind his desk.

Benny's first words to me were, "Why are you getting up from the desk? Don't you have more work to do?"

I replied, "It's your desk, Sir, and I am just getting out of your way."

He motioned for me to go sit down again. He took a seat in one of the chairs in front of the desk. I could see he was moving pretty slowly and carefully, but he looked good.

He said, "Well, I hear you haven't burned the place down yet, and all of the employees don't completely hate you."

I replied, "I hope not, Sir."

Then he said, "The other day, I was taking a secret walk on the more remote part of the beach, and I saw a sign showing me where I could find fresh lemonade. It made me thirsty."

All I could do was smile, and he did the same, and then we started laughing hysterically.

But then Benny got all serious, let some silence go by, and he said, "Look. I can't put you back up in a lifeguard tower, because everyone at this entire resort thinks you are running the place. But I also can't give you my office here because you are about to leave and go back to school."

I replied, "I understand."

Then he said, "But I would deeply appreciate it if you could continue doing what you are doing for a couple more weeks while I try to ease myself back in. Then I will oversee everything being closed up for the season myself."

I responded, "That's fine, Sir."

There was another pause, and he said, "I cannot fully express the amount of respect I have for you."

There was a certain tone in his words where I felt I might tear up if I let it happen, and it looked to me that Benny was on the verge of doing the same.

I said to him, "You don't need to say anything. I was just living up to my responsibilities, as certain people want to see from me, and that I want to see from myself."

He nodded like he understood everything behind my words.

He got up from his chair, and I guess was going to leave. He got halfway out of the office door, and turned around with a huge smirk on his face, and said, "You DO REALIZE, that the whole heart attack thing was just meant to be your lifeguard final exam, right?"

We both smiled on the verge of laughing again, and I replied, "Yes, I figured as much, Sir."

He simply replied, "Well you passed." Then he walked away before I could respond at all.

My final days at The Lake passed quickly. Before I knew it, it was my last day. I had already turned the office back over to Benny. However, out of routine, I still did my usual 'rounds' around the resort, checking in on the restaurants and everything. Whenever someone asked me for something, I replied, "Benny's back." Much to my surprise, I often got a look of disappointment and dismay. (*Don't tell Benny this. It will be our secret*) Honestly, I had a ton of respect for Benny and how he did his job. I got a very close-up look at how difficult his job was. Having seen all of the difficulties, demands, and complexities, I felt Benny had done a wonderful job as Director of The Lake. I had filled-in for only a short time, but Benny had been doing the job for MANY YEARS. I knew he belonged in that position.

After I had checked on everything inside the cafeteria, I took a seat outside at one of the brand-new picnic tables that had arrived. I was a bit bummed that I would not be able to see-through my outdoor dining expansion. However, Jonathan was going forward with all of my new initiatives, and Benny would take over the implementation next season.

I sat at the table staring out at the lake. I had the same feeling that I had when I was leaving the farm after farm camp. It was that feeling of having found a place where I belonged. I felt my efforts had been meaningful. I didn't want it to end, and I didn't want to leave.

But school was starting up again. I had no choice. I couldn't believe I was still in high school. I felt so much older than that. Then I started to get sad. I knew what would come next. I would go back to school, and within days, start acting like a child again. School seemed to bring out the worst in me. Each summer I seemed to become an adult, and then each school year, I would go back to being a child.

The adult world was very empowering for me. I was able to rise higher without the enclosures and limitations of school. It felt like in school we were being taught what to think, and to follow the leader. But in real life out in the world, I was learning HOW to think, and how to BE THE LEADER.

Out in the world, I was afraid of nothing. But at school I was pretty much a coward, just wanting to not make any waves, and stay invisible.

Sitting at that table, in that moment, I swore to myself that if I ever was in a position of power to create change someday, that I was going to change how the school approached education. But until then, I would have to play the game as it was laid out. I was not looking forward to it. But such is life.

My mom was coming to pick me up that evening. Once I had done my last checks of all the facilities in the resort, I officially inside my own head, relieved myself of duty. I was done. I told Eric I wanted to enjoy one last meal with him, and just hang out with him until my mom arrived.

We both chose to get the awesome burgers we had come to enjoy so much. We ate them outside on "my" new picnic tables. We kept the conversation light, and didn't want to make each other sad. We didn't go to the same school, so we knew we wouldn't see each other again for a while. When we were done eating, I told Eric that we should go and say goodbye to Benny.

We walked over to the main office and went inside Benny's office. It was surreal for me to be back in Benny's office as just a 'nobody' who didn't work there or have any responsibility or authority. It was like things had come full-circle. It felt like Benny's office again. It was like all of my time in there was just a dream or something.

Benny acted like he had been waiting for us, because he told us to have a seat. He looked like he had some kind of announcement to make. I was thinking in my head, "*What now?*" But it was good.

He started by saying, "I'm obviously not making you guys pay for the sailboat. I'm going to pay you guys for all of the regular wages you earned this summer at your jobs."

Eric's face lit up like a Christmas tree.

Benny looked over at me, and almost with a look of shame, said, "There is no way I can pay you for what you did this summer. What I owe you is incalculable. I wouldn't even know what I owe you." He continued, "BUT I am going to pay you for all of your 'lifeguard hours' worked the entire summer."

I didn't have much of a reaction to this, because I was not expecting any extra pay, nor was I really wanting it. Yes, in the back of my mind I questioned my own sanity of not wanting full payment for everything. But for some reason, I just didn't want it. I felt that everything I gained and experienced, was beyond any payment, and any payment might even cheapen what I had learned, experienced, and accomplished.

I said to Benny, "It's okay, I wasn't expecting anything. But I will take my lifeguard pay, and I want it to go to Eric."

Eric swung his head over to me in shock. Benny looked stunned and confused as well. I didn't look at Eric. I kept eye contact with Benny and said, "Eric deserves it, and I know he and his mom need it more than me."

Benny said to me, "Are you sure young man?"

I said, "I'm absolutely certain."

Benny dug my check out of the envelope he was going to hand me, and told me to sign the back of the check, and endorse it to Eric. I did. I handed the check back to Benny. Benny slid my check into Eric's envelope, and gave the envelope to Eric.

Eric opened the envelope and looked at both of the checks. When he saw the amount of both checks, he looked stunned and he started tearing up. He said, "Now I can buy school clothes, any school supplies I will need, and all kinds of things. Plus, I can help my mom."

After Eric said that, I think Benny fully understood why I had done what I did. Although my family didn't have much money, and I certainly had zero money for myself, we had enough to get by. I would still get a couple of new outfits for school, and we would be fine. But Eric was in a different circumstance. I knew they had a very rough money situation. I felt maybe this was a great way to push Eric into the new school year on a positive note.

Eric was trying to keep from crying, but Benny and I saw how affected he was by getting all of this money unexpectedly. Benny and I both looked at each other and smiled. We both felt good about what we had done.

I noticed a bunch of staff workers lined up outside of Benny's office waiting to talk with him. I pointed to the line of people and said, "Well, that's a familiar sight for me, and I know what that means. So, we will throw ourselves out of your office now so you can get back to work." Benny laughed.

Eric and I both got up and started walking out. Benny stood up and said, "Thank you. Really. Thank you. For everything."

I just gave him a military salute and walked out. Eric gave him a little wave and mouthed "Thank you" to him. We walked out of the main office and outside into the parking lot.

There was nothing to do now but say goodbye to Eric while we waited for our moms to pick us up. I looked at him, and before I could say anything he said, "What you did back there for me. I can't even." I cut him off, and said, "What I did back there was what I wanted to do. I know you will make the best of it." Eric just nodded, trying not to cry.

I felt it was time for the most difficult part. I looked at him and said, "I guess this is bye for now."

Eric replied, "I'm afraid I won't see you again. I'm afraid you will end up with amazing opportunities, and be off on your life adventure, and I won't see you anymore."

I looked at him in the eyes and said, "Eric, I promise you that whatever happens to me in the future, I am going to make sure that YOU are a part of it, for certain."

He smiled, and I think that made him feel better. I meant it. Deep down, I knew special things were possibly going to happen at some point, and I promised myself, let alone him, that I was going to include him.

My mom pulled into the parking area. Eric's mom was not far behind. Eric and I saw this. We hugged, but no words were spoken. Then I put my hands on his shoulders and said, "Until next time."

I turned away and walked to my mom's car. I got in, and we drove away. I was grateful that my mom was not talkative. I really needed silence. I needed to think, or not think, but I needed silence. We were almost home when the silence was broken and she said, "Remember, we have to go school shopping for you this coming week."

I laughed and said, "Yeah mom."

Then she added, "You can pick out a brand-new pair of sneakers also."

I just smirked and said, "Okay mom, cool."

When we arrived home, I told her I wanted to walk down to the park first, and that I would take my suitcase inside later."

She smiled amusedly as if she was expecting this.

I started walking down the street toward the park. As I passed by Mr. Wilkens's old house, I gave it a wave, then a salute, as a sign of respect for him.

When I arrived at the park, the bench that I always sat at, seemed slightly smaller than usual for some reason, but I knew it was the same bench.

As I sat on the park bench and reflected upon my summer at The Lake, I felt nothing but gratitude for the adults in my life who had forced me to step up and reach toward my full potential as a person who would not shrink from his destiny. I was being shown, taught, and groomed, to live a meaningful life.

To further enjoy this series, "**Living A Meaningful Life**," be sure to check out the other books in the series below:

Book #1: ***The Bench:*** *Living A Meaningful Life*
Book #2: ***The Farm:*** *Living A Meaningful Life*
Book #3: ***The Lake:*** *Living A Meaningful Life*
Book #4: ***The Favor:*** *Living A Meaningful Life*
Book #5: ***The Promise:*** *Living A Meaningful Life*
Book #6: ***The Sacrifice:*** *Living A Meaningful Life*
Book #7: ***The Challenge:*** *Living A Meaningful Life*
Book #8: ***The Wedding:*** *Living A Meaningful Life*
Book #9: ***The Crew:*** *Living A Meaningful Life*

Acknowledgments

Thank you Sarah Delamere Hurding for your editorial assistance, encouragement, and endless support.

Thanks to all of my clients and benefactors who have supported my mission of helping people become greater, stronger, more self-empowered, enlightened, and free of pain.

Thank you, Enya, for your genius and creative musical inspiration.

ABOUT THE AUTHOR

Brian Hunter is an American Author and Life Coach based in Los Angeles, California. However, Brian started life with a rural upbringing, surrounded by small towns, farms, lakes, and the peace of nature. Brian is the author of the "Living A Meaningful Life" series, *Surviving Life: Contemplations Of The Soul, EVOLVE, Heal Me, Rising To Greatness, The Hunter Equation, Aliens,* and *The Walk-In*. His books have sold around the world and have been Best Sellers within their genres. Brian was acknowledged as being intuitive as a child, and then later in life was attributed as having psychic abilities. Brian has worked with people from all over the world, including celebrities and captains of industry. Brian was an original cast member of the TV series pilot *Missing Peace*, in which psychics worked with detectives to solve cold cases. He has also worked as an actor and model in Hollywood, and been featured in various movie and TV productions. Brian's current focus is on his writing and life coaching work, helping clients from all walks of life.

www.brianhunterhelps.com

ALSO, BY BRIAN HUNTER

The Bench: Living A Meaningful Life, is the first book in the "Living A Meaningful Life" series. *The Bench* is a collection of four epic tales that intertwine into one. These heart-warming life-stories evoke emotions, memories, and yearnings from deep within that remind us of how loving, meaningful, and hopeful life can be. Through struggle and tragedy, *The Bench* shows us that we can still learn, grow, and eventually thrive. This book brings you back to your childhood roots, and will touch your soul, while making you laugh and cry. *The Bench* reminds us of what is most important in life.

The Farm: Living A Meaningful Life, is the second book in the "Living A Meaningful Life" series. *The Farm* is the follow up book to *The Bench*, and continues the journey for the main character, as well as some new ones that are sure to become favorites. This time, the setting takes place on a farm, where a group of teens are stuck together, learning more life lessons, and learning more about themselves. This installment is full of laughs, tears, heartfelt moments, and answers some questions left by *The Bench*.

The Favor: *Living A Meaningful Life*, is Book #4 in the "Living A Meaningful Life" series. In this, the most pivotal and climactic installment of the series yet, the main character must make sacrifices for those who mean the most to him, as he faces life shattering losses, and must summon all of his strength, inner character, and utilize the life lessons taught to him by his mentors. He meets the moment for which his mentors have been preparing and grooming him for. This book has a particularly meaningful focus on dealing with grief from loss, especially when you find yourself alone in life after losing someone closest to you.

The Promise: *Living A Meaningful Life*, is Book #5 in the "Living A Meaningful Life" series. In this very emotional, inspiring, and touching installment of the series, the main character must once again make changes to his life in order to honor promises made. He realizes that sacrifices made, to honor promises given, can result in the greatest gifts that life has to offer. *The Promise* will stir within you deep emotions, and leave you contemplating your own life choices and possibilities. When we have the courage and discipline to 'do the right things,' for the right reasons, we are richly rewarded in ways that we cannot even imagine. There are plenty of tears in this one, but they are tears of joy. You will also enjoy an abundance of laughs, as you experience the banter between the characters we have come to know and love.

The Sacrifice: *Living A Meaningful Life,* is Book #6 in the "Living A Meaningful Life" series. In this very emotional, inspiring, and touching installment of the series, the main character and his family must once again 'do the right things,' and make huge sacrifices for the benefit of the community they love and swore to support. Huge sacrifices made, can result in huge blessings given. There are deeply moving ups and downs in this one, but you will enjoy an abundance of laughs, as you experience the banter between the characters we have come to know and love.

The Challenge: Living A Meaningful Life, is Book #7 in the "Living A Meaningful Life" series. In this very amusing, inspiring, and touching installment of the series, the young star of the series finally gets his chance to prove himself. He must endure trials and tribulations to see if he has what it takes to secure his place within the family dynasty. This is one of the high points of the series, and sets the direction for the next phase of the series. This installment is full of fun moments, and allows the reader to truly enjoy the teen who has become the favorite character of the series. You will enjoy an abundance of laughs, as you experience the banter between the characters we have come to know and love.

The Wedding: Living A Meaningful Life, is Book #8 in the "Living A Meaningful Life" series. In this very amusing and touching installment of the series, our favorite couple finally tie the knot. But that is by no means a spoiler, as there are some twists and turns involved. Our favorite young star does not disappoint in delivering to us more of his antics and genius. In one of the most hilarious moments in the series, there is a father/son discussion regarding our favorite teen "coming of age," and having his first girlfriend.

The Crew: Living A Meaningful Life, is Book #9 in the "Living A Meaningful Life" series. This very amusing, inspiring, and touching installment, gives us a closer look into Rudy's huge inner circle of friends, and their hilarious antics. This installment is another high point of the series, as it chronicles Rudy's growing success, but also features a very emotional event which rocks his world. How Rudy handles this "event" will prove him worthy of his destiny. This is a highly emotional installment, and will leave you changed as a person.

Surviving Life: Contemplations Of The Soul is a unique and powerful book full of compassion and empathy, which combines the issues of what hurts us the most, with thoughts and advice meant to empower us toward happiness and independence. *Surviving Life* is medicine for the soul. It guides us through our deepest pains and weaknesses, and leads us to a place of self-empowerment, inspiration, strength, and hope. The topics covered are raw, diverse, and very practical. *Surviving Life* includes many subjects, and answers many questions, such as, "What is your purpose on this planet," "When you think nobody loves you," "How can you feel good," as well as practical advice on battling depression, suicide, and figuring out who you truly are. *Surviving Life* is a practical and contemplative manual for people of all ages, and the perfect book for gifting to those who need guidance and love.

EVOLVE is a cutting-edge, unique, powerful, and practical personal transformation self-help improvement book, which examines human life and all of its issues from a unique futuristic approach with a touch of humor. A selection of topics include: healing from personal losses and traumas, coping with sadness and depression, moving past fear that others use to control, manipulate, and abuse you, clarity in thinking, advanced communication skills, evolving your relationships, exploring the meaning of life, how everything in the Universe is connected, developing your psychic ability, and a little discussion about aliens possibly living among us. Yes, there is everything, which is all directly tied back to your own personal life.

Heal Me is a powerful and touching book that will pull at your heartstrings, give you practical advice on overcoming a variety of life traumas, and will put you on the road to recovery and healing. *Heal Me* examines such issues as the death of a loved one, loss of a pet, suicide, anxiety, addiction, life failures, major life mistakes, broken relationships, abuse, sexual assault, self-esteem, living in a toxic world surrounded by toxic people, loneliness, and many other issues. This is a self-care book written in a very loving, practical, and informative way that you can gift to yourself, family, young people, and friends, as a gesture of love, support, and hope.

Rising To Greatness is a self-help book that takes you on a step-by-step transformation, from the ashes of being broken and lost, to the greatness of self-empowerment, accomplishment, and happiness. This book includes such topics as developing your sense of self, eliminating fear from your life, mastering your emotions, self-discipline and motivation, communication skills, and so much more.

LIVING A MEANINGFUL LIFE BOOK SERIES INSTALLMENT SYNOPSIS

This is a series for adults, but has many themes, stories, and lessons, that would be enjoyed by a teen audience as well. Through its down-to-Earth, emotional, and touching storylines, the series shows the importance of developing self-empowerment, and a person's own deep character, through mentors, self-work, and 'soul-families.' The main theme is that of always 'doing the right things,' as a way of living a meaningful life. All installments within this series feature characters of all ages, from children to older adults. The series is neutral on religion and politics. There are tears of sadness, tears of joy, and lots of laughs. This is a series that changes lives.

Book #1, *The Bench*, is an important book that lays the foundation for the series. This installment provides the background for important mentors and characters featured in the series. This installment covers much of the main character's childhood, and provides important lessons learned, as well as a number of the back-stories referred to later on in the series.

Book #2, *The Farm*, is the more "juvenile" installment of the series, but is a critical book that provides the background on the most important mentor of the series, as well as many of the back-stories for the series. In this installment, the main character is a young teen. This is also a "coming of age" installment, where the main character realizes the meaning of leadership, and the importance of having a mentor.

Book #3, *The Lake*, is the installment where the main character transforms from a teenage child to a highly dynamic teenage young adult. This installment is a major turning-point in his life. His destiny is decided in this installment, but he doesn't know it yet.

Book #4, *The Favor*, is the most pivotal installment of the series. Everything changes, and the main character's future is laid out before him. Highly emotional and intense installment. The main character is now a young adult, and a new future star of the series is introduced.

Book #5, *The Promise*, is the 'relief' installment after the intensity of Book #4. The main character must accept his new life, and live up to his promises and obligations. The new rising star of the series begins to become very prominent.

Book #6, *The Sacrifice*, reminds us that things can always change in an instant. This installment tests the resolve of the main character, as he must draw upon the lessons taught to him by his mentors, as he faces his greatest challenge yet.

Book #7, *The Challenge*, is the next most pivotal installment, where the previously rising star of the series solidifies his prominence as THE star of the series. This installment exhibits the power that people can have if they dare to rise up and soar like an Eagle.

Book #8, *The Wedding,* gives us what we have been wanting and waiting for. But in addition to that, this is the "coming of age" installment for the young star of the series, who all of a sudden, blossoms into a young man with his own independence and ideas, as most older teenagers do. The young star continues to surpass all expectations.

Book #9, *The Crew,* gives us a closer look into Rudy's huge inner circle of friends, and their antics. This installment is another high point in the series, as it chronicles Rudy's growing success, but also a very emotional event which rocks his world. How Rudy handles this "event" will prove him worthy of his destiny. Highly emotional installment.

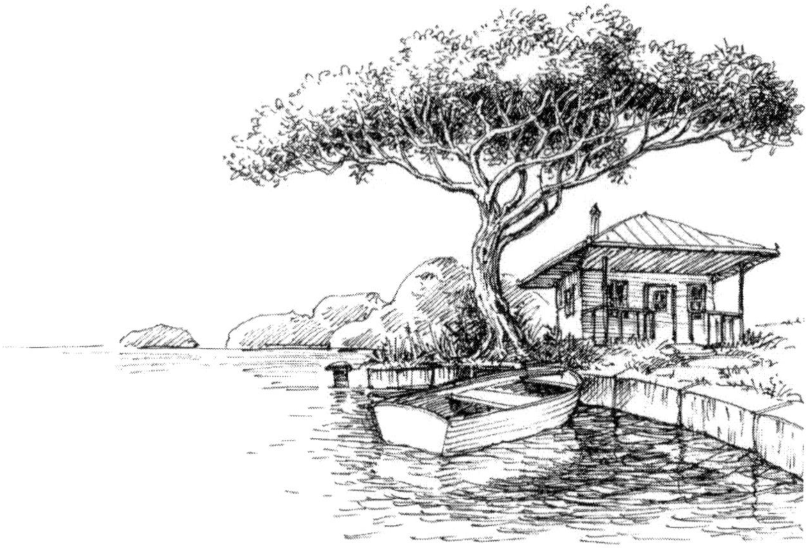